Sir Granville Bantock

Round the World with a Gaiety Girl

Sir Granville Bantock

Round the World with a Gaiety Girl

ISBN/EAN: 9783744729765

Printed in Europe, USA, Canada, Australia, Japan

Cover: Foto ©Andreas Hilbeck / pixelio.de

More available books at **www.hansebooks.com**

"THE DRAMA BIRTHDAY BOOK."

COMPILED BY

PERCY S. PHILLIPS.

Foolscap 8vo, art linen, 3s. 6d.; morocco, 10s. 6d.

The Daily Telegraph says :
"An interesting variant in the way of natal literature is the ' Drama Birthday Book,' which Mr. Percy S. Phillips has compiled and dedicated to Miss Annie Hughes. The little volume is prettily decorated both inside and out, and contains witty and sentimental quotations from the works of a very large number of modern playwrights."

The Stage says :
" 'The Drama Birthday Book,' compiled by Percy S. Phillips, and dedicated to Miss Annie Hughes, is really a charming little work, that should find ready sale at this time of year. Each page, too, is illustrated in quaint and pleasing fashion. This is a volume I can certainly recommend to my friends."

The Era says :
"The volume is daintily got up and brightly illustrated, and would make an appropriate gift-book to members of the profession."

The Globe says :
"Every printed page has pictorial illustrations, most of them very quaint and taking. The binding is neat, and altogether the little book, which is dedicated to Miss Annie Hughes, is likely to have a wide popularity."

JOHN MACQUEEN,

HASTINGS HOUSE, NORFOLK STREET, STRAND.

Round the World

with

"A Gaiety Girl"

POPULAR SONGS FROM

THE SHOP GIRL.

GAIETY THEATRE.

"I WANT YER, MA HONEY."

Fay Templeton's charming Coon Carol.

Sung by Miss Ellaline Terriss.

Refrain.

I want yer, ma honey, yes, I want yer mighty badly;
I'm a longin' for yer daily,
'Cos I love yer mighty madly;
So come back to please me—don't try to tease me,
'Cos I want yer, ma honey, yes, I want yer, want yer, want yer,
I want yer, ma honey, yes, I do!

"THE LITTLE MAD'MOISELLE."

By Leslie Stuart. *Sung by* Seymour Hicks.

Refrain.

And when she says, "Je suis Française," just smile like this!
And then this pretty little Mad'moiselle begins to parlez
    and the tale to tell.
And when she says, "Ah! twiggez vous?" say, "Oui,
    ma belle,
Very chiccy, very tricky, vous trez thicky, Mad'moiselle!"

"LOUSIANA LOU."

By Leslie Stuart. *Sung by* Miss Ellaline Terriss.

Refrain.

Lou, Lou, I lub you, I lub you, dat's true;
Don't cry, don't sigh, I'll see you in de mornin'.
Dream, dream, dream ob me, and I'll dream ob you,
My Lousiana, Lousiana, Lousiana Lou!

"AND HER GOLDEN HAIR WAS HANGING DOWN HER BACK."

By Adrian Ross and Felix McGlennon.

Sung by Seymour Hicks.

Refrain—But, oh, Flo! such a change you know,
    When she left the village she was shy;
    But alas, and alack! she's gone back
    With a naughty little twinkle in her eye!

POPULAR "GAIETY" DANCES.

Lousiana Lou Waltz.	By Carl Kiefert.
Her Golden Hair Barn Dance.	By Karl Kaps.
Her Golden Hair Waltz.	By Harry Wood.

} *2/- net, each.*

—

Francis Day & Hunter, 195 Oxford St., London, W.
T. B. Harms & Co., 18 East Twenty-Second Street,
New York, U.S.A.
And all Musicsellers.

From a Photo by Hana.]

GEORGE EDWARDES.

[44 Strand.

Round the World

with

"A Gaiety Girl"

By

Granville Bantock

and

F. G. Aflalo

Illustrated from Photographs

London
John Macqueen
Hastings House, Norfolk Street, W.C.
1896

Foreword

BY way of apology for the looseness of this short farrago, it seems fair to all parties to state that it was, in the first place, strung together in the hope of providing a little souvenir of our delightful trip.

As books are bought nowadays almost as indiscriminately as they are made, it is hoped that the "general reader" will pardon the introduction of one or two little personal anecdotes and allusions.

LONDON, *March* 1896.

Contents

CONTENTS

CONTENTS

List of Illustrations

Note.—The illustration on the cover of this book is reproduced with the kind permission of Messrs. Waterlow & Sons, Limited.

The Atlantic

11

The Atlantic

Waterloo—Southampton—The *Berlin*—Bad Start—
Stoppage in Mid Ocean—Concert—Arrival at
New York.

A T 3.45 P.M., on the 1st of September
1894, we left the platform at Waterloo. Or rather, that was the precise hour
for which our departure was advertised,
though we were somewhat delayed by the
dense crowd of friends who had assembled
to see us off, not to mention the usual
requirements of the L. & S.-W. R. Co. in the
nature of a little margin of fifteen minutes
or so. This was, however, a welcome
respite for those about to part. It was

13

a lovely afternoon indeed, though, with so
many friends left behind to think about, and
so much of novelty before us, we had no
appreciation for the beautiful tints of early
autumn which lay on the Berkshire wolds, or
the endless stretches of evergreen Hamp-
shire pines through which we were flying.
Perhaps, too, the eye was a little dimmed,
whether by tears or by Mr. Edwardes' lavish
hospitality, which followed us to the very
docks, it boots not to say. At length Southampton was reached; selves and baggage
were without more ado conveyed aboard the
good ship *Berlin*; and Mr. Edwardes and
a few other friends had to take leave of us.

The *Berlin* weighed anchor shortly before
eight, and steamed majestically out of Southampton water and into a dense fog, which
kept her anchored in the fortunately calm
Solent until near dawn. Dog-tired many of

us were after the day's excitement, but the heat was so intense as to prevent any but the poorest attempt at sleep; and when the donkey-engines brayed and the screw revolved afresh at 4.30 next morning, many were glad to go on deck. The coast is soon lost sight of, only reappearing late the same afternoon, when a glimpse of the Lizard and low-lying Manacle Land, and a still later peep at the Scillies, are the last we are to see of the old country for a twelvemonth and more. The heat, still intense at midday, began to moderate somewhat in the afternoon, which was agreeable; and the sea was making up its mind for a romp on the third day, which was not. Fortunately it abandoned that intention until some, at all events, had got their "sea-legs."

Perhaps this is a convenient place to enumerate our company as at first constituted. It consisted (under the management of Mr. J. A. E. Malone) of Miss Decima Moore, Miss Juliette Nesville, Miss Maud Hobson, Miss Blanche Massey, Mrs. Edmund Phelps, Miss Grace Palotta, Miss Florence Lloyd, Miss Cissie Fitzgerald, Miss Ethel Selwyn, Miss Sophie Elliott, Miss Marie Yorke, Miss Maggie Crossland, Miss May Lucas, and Miss Lucy Murray; Messrs. Harry Monkhouse, Fred Kaye, Louis Bradfield, Charles Ryley, Leedham Bantock, Cecil Hope, Fritz Rimma, E. G. Woodhouse, and Granville Bantock as musical director. Mr. Arthur Hope subsequently joined us in New York.

The "sweep" occasioned the usual amusement, which was still greater of an evening when the numbers were sold by auction. A slight hitch occurred that night in the machinery, in consequence of which we had to lie-to for several hours. The only ship with which we had hitherto fallen in was the *Normannia*, which had passed us close on the starboard, herself bound for Southampton; but on the occasion of our enforced stoppage, we were passed and spoken by the German ship *Trave*, bound for New York. We refused her proffered assistance, so she proceeded on her course; so that Miss Nesville, who left Southampton at least a day later than ourselves, reached America before us.

During the next day or two the Atlantic grew mischievous, with the result that more than one place was vacant at the breakfast-table. Smooth or rough, however, the ship's run averaged 325 knots, varying between 258 and 370.

On the sixth day from port, one of the company was heard asking loudly for the bathroom, to which a benevolent steward kindly conducted him.

When we had been at sea a week, equilibrium was sufficiently restored for us to venture on giving a concert in aid of the Seamen's Widows Fund, and a great success it was pronounced. The programme, as much as we can remember of it, was as follows :—

PART I.

Overture . . "A Gaiety Girl" .		Mr. G. BANTOCK
Song . . . "Ritournelle" .		. Miss LLOYD
Song . . "Some do it this way"		Mr. BRADFIELD
Recitation		. Miss HOBSON
Song . {"When your pride has had a tumble"		Miss PALOTTA
Song . . "There is none like to thee"		Miss MOORE

PART II.

Song {"The Dandy Coloured Coon"		Mr. BRADFIELD
Song		Miss PALOTTA
A few words by		. Mr. KAYE
Song		. Miss MOORE
Song		Mr. BRADFIELD

Next day, being Sunday, divine service

was held in the morning. Wet Sundays are not specially reserved for those on land. This particular Sabbath was wretched: pouring rain, and a high sea the whole afternoon, and, to crown all, a dense fog in the evening. To be even becalmed in a fog such as we ran into before getting clear of the Wight is bad enough for most tastes; but fog together with a strong head sea baffles description. As often happens, however, it had a beneficial effect on the troubled waters, which calmed down wonderfully during our remaining four and twenty hours in the open.

Next afternoon we picked up the pilot, and the fog soon lifted, discovering to our eager gaze the low-lying shore of Long Island. "Eager gaze" seems the proper expression on the threshold of a new continent; though, as a matter of fact, the recently perturbed waters had kept the majority below, so that this first glimpse of America was perhaps not duly appreciated.

What did attract the attention of all before many hours had elapsed was a triple thunder-storm, such as few of us had ever before witnessed, which burst with fury over the land as we were running for New York harbour. The lightnings flashed through the darkness in a very beautiful manner, though whether we should have appreciated a spectacle of this description a thousand miles from the shore is another matter. The storm, however, soon abated, and the *Berlin* came to her moorings in Quarantine Bay, where she lay all night. It was here that we got our first glimpse of the distant lights on Brooklyn Bridge and the Liberty Statue.

About ten next morning the customs officers boarded us in a launch, and, before

WRS

J. A. E. MALONE.

the *Berlin* was suffered to proceed to the wharf, we had to sign declaration papers. Why so much time and temper must needs be lost in this proceeding is not very evident, since all baggage is afterwards subjected to a most searching examination at the quay.

All good things, however, even the importunities of customs officials, must come to an end, and at last we got ashore; and a party proceeded straight to Ashland House (Fourth Avenue and Twenty-fourth Street), where they engaged rooms, on the American plan, at a weekly charge of fourteen dollars.

Early the same afternoon we assembled by appointment at Daly's Theatre, where we were introduced to Mr. Daly himself; and next day our rehearsals of *A Gaiety Girl* began in earnest, and took up the best part of a week before the first performance.

New York and the Eastern States

23

New York and the Eastern States

Lights of the City—The Lambs' Club—Great Heat—
First Performance — Illness of Monkhouse—
Sunday Excursions—Niagara—Impressions of
New York City—Harlem—Heavy Snowfall—
Boston — Washington — Wretched Theatre —
The Menagerie — Grand Buildings — Overlook
Hills—Brooklyn—We start West.

OUR stay in New York city extended over
a couple of months. The first few
days we were busy with rehearsals, and not
until the 18th did we give our first performance. With less time for sightseeing than
some could have wished, we yet contrived
in the interval to visit Chinatown and

Harlem, and to see a few of the shows; among which memory recalls a professional *matinée* at the Broadway Theatre, when De Wolff Hopper gave an excellent performance as Dr. Syntax; a very poor Roof Garden concert at the Casino; Kastor and Bial's variety show; Hanlon's " Fantasma " at the People's Theatre; " 1492 " at the Garden Theatre; Huber's Dime Museum, and several besides.

In the intervals of work and suchlike instructive recreation, we were overwhelmed with the hospitality of the Lambs' Club, where we met De Wolff Hopper, Eugene Cowles, Marius, and others. Many of us were made members of this most hospitable of Bohemian clubs; and one evening, a "Gambol," we shall not soon forget, the *pièce de résistance* being " The Transgressor in the Bauble Shop," after which Bradfield

NEW YORK

contributed "Some do it this way" and "The Little Nipper."

LAMBS' THEATRE.

SUNDAY EVENING, NOV. 4, 1894.

DE WOLF HOPPER, Collie.

Grand Opening of the Regular Season with the following novel list of Irregularities.

1. What ho, from the country, our Hay-Seed Shepherd,

CLAY M. GREENE,

Will deliver a short lecture on travel, entitled :

"A DELIGHTFUL BIGAMY."

2. And by way of variety, and by permission of the Queen and the rest of the pack,

LOUIS BRADFIELD,

Of the "Gaiety Girl" Co. Aided and abetted by a brother conspirator,

GRANVILLE BANTOCK.

27

ROUND THE WORLD

3. The Albion's friend, gentle and persuasive,

WILTON LACKAYE,

Will recite.

---

4. Here comes the Bostonian, so called because he hails
   from Chicago ; but whatever his native place, his home
   is in our hearts, and his name is

EUGENE COWLES.

---

5. To be followed by Messrs.

BROOKS & DENTON,

The only two known mortals who can cheer and not
inebriate us with a Banjo.

---

6. Here is a good place for

CHAUNCEY OLCOTT,

The Irish tenor, the Irish artist, the Irish gentleman, but
who, nevertheless, will sing in English.

---

7. The Olio will conclude with the King of Vaudevillains,
   who will extract things from his budget while you wait.

CHARLES J. ROSS.

TEN MINUTES FOR THOUGHT AND STIMULANT.

NEW YORK

The Collie has the honour to announce that he will present for the first time on any stage SYDNEY ROSEN-FELD'S original compilation of *fin-de-siècle* literature, entitled :

A TRANSGRESSOR

——IN A——

BAUBLE SHOP.

With the following cast :

Lord Clive	. DE WOLF HOPPER
Jessie Keber . . .	JOHN C. BUCKSTONE
Old Man Keber	NELSON WHEATCROFT
The Rev. Mr. Meredith . . .	GRANT STEWART
Stoach, under an *alias* . .	. HUGO TOLAND

At this point, the intellectual entertainment being over, and the audience intoxicated with pleasure, homeopathically indulges in counter-intoxication downstairs, and enables the present House Committee to make a record. They will be summoned for

SUPPER AND INSTALLATION OF OFFICERS,

and a few things of that sort that will carry the general joy into the wee hours.

During the first part of our stay in New York city it was intensely hot, the atmosphere, especially before the frequent storms, being as sultry as that of a Turkish bath. This was not without its effect on several of the company, who took it in turns to be laid up; though the first serious change through illness did not occur until our week at the Harlem Opera House, when Monkhouse fell ill, and Bradfield undertook the rôle of "Dr. Brierly."

In the dressing-rooms, too, this heat made itself felt in a most disagreeable manner, for the grease paints refused to remain *in situ*, and nothing but frequent application met the difficulty.

The first performance, on the 18th, was a great success, and the next day's papers were unanimous in praise of *A Gaiety Girl*.

NEW YORK

The cast was as follows :—

Captain Goldfield .	Officers	. Mr. CHARLES RYLEY
Major Barclay .	of	. . Mr. FRED KAYE
Bobbie Rivers .	the	Mr. W. LOUIS BRADFIELD
Harry Fitz Warren	Life	. . Mr. ARTHUR HOPE
Ronny Farquhar .	Guards	. . Mr. CECIL HOPE

Sir Lewis Gray (Judge of the Divorce Court) } Mr. LEEDHAM BANTOCK

Lance (Goldfield's Servant) .   Mr. E. C. WOODHOUSE

Auguste (Bathing Attendant)   .   . Mr. FRITZ RIMMA

—— AND ——

Dr. Montague Brierly .   .   Mr. HARRY MONKHOUSE

Rose Brierly (his Daughter)   .   Miss DECIMA MOORE

Lady Edytha Aldwyn	Society	Miss MARIE YORKE
Miss Gladys Stourton	Ladies	Miss SOPHIE ELLIOTT
Hon. Daisy Ormsbury		Miss ETHEL SELWYN

Lady Gray (Wife of Sir Lewis) .   Mrs. EDMUND PHELPS

Alma Somerset	Girls	Miss BLANCHE MASSEY
Cissy Verner	of the	Miss FLORENCE LLOYD
Haidee Walton	"Gaiety"	Miss CISSIE FITZGERALD
Ethel Hawthorn		Miss GRACE PALOTTA

Lady Virginia Forrest .   .   .   Miss MAUD HOBSON

Mina (Maid to Lady Virginia) . Miss JULIETTE NESVILLE

The *PAS SEUL* in Act 1, by Miss CISSIE FITZGERALD.

In Act 2, a *CARNIVAL DANCE* by Mesdames
MAGGIE CROSSLAND, LUCY MURRAY, and MAY LUCAS.

Act 1. Pleasure Grounds, in View of Windsor.
Act 2. Nice, with View of Monte Carlo.

For the next eight weeks we kept hard at work, giving eight performances weekly, Wednesdays and Saturdays being *matinée* days.

Save in Chicago, where we had to perform, Sunday was of course the favourite day for excursions, one of the prettiest here being by steamboat up the Hudson River as far as West Point, returning by the train along west shore.

Another delightful Sunday outing was by ferry to New Jersey, thence by car to Hoboken, electric car to North Bergen and Hudson Heights, and back by train to the ferry at Weehauken.

On our sixth Sunday in the city, two of the party—the only two, by the way, who "did" the Falls—were off to Niagara, *via* Albany, Utica, Syracuse, Rochester, and Batavia.

Buffalo was reached in the afternoon, and our enterprising travellers arrived just in time to see the Falls before darkness set in, leaving again the same evening, and arriving in New York before eleven next morning, which was quick work.

Neither seems to have regretted this flying visit, which ran into more dollars than hours.

We were shown every kindness during our stay in New York city,—as, indeed, where were we not!—and afforded every facility for seeing over many interesting institutions, such as the Naval Dockyard at Brooklyn and the *New York* cruiser; the Fire Department, where an engine was harnessed for our benefit in a few seconds, and where, on another occasion, we witnessed a remarkably smart fire-drill; the head of the Liberty Statue; the offices of the *New York Times*, with their wonderful linotype

machines ; Edison's fascinating laboratory
at Orange, where we made a more thorough
acquaintance with the marvellous kinetoscope
and phonograph, in the former of which we
saw our three carnival dancers at work ; Black-
well's Island, with its Hospital, Penitentiary,
and Asylums, and the gangs of male and female
convicts, soberly clad in black and white ; the
Morgue, where the corpses were packed away
in ice; and a number of other sights, the mere
enumeration of which would fill a chapter.

After a most enjoyable stay, we left New
York, at the close of which engagement
Miss Nesville left us and returned to
England.

It must be confessed that the memories
of this city are not all roseate. There
is a singular combination of magnificence
and primitive patchwork. The chess-board
laid, regularly numbered streets lack the

picturesque windings of old-world cities; the fifteen-storeyed buildings convey a general impression of hopeless overcrowding. As for the paving, Broadway is more backward in this respect than was Cheapside ten years ago. A rainy day here is, in consequence of this, something to be dreaded. The elevated railway, though doubtless a great convenience, is at the same time a constant source of annoyance, and shuts out the sky in a most unpleasant manner.

Another thing that struck us, was the comparative dulness of New York, though something of this may be attributed to Dr. Parkhurst's crusade, which was then revealing such terrible secrets. Gaiety, indeed, there was none, though things brightened to some extent during the elections, which resulted in the downthrow of Tammany Hall by the Republican party. There is a want of security in these American cities which will hardly be credited at home. As an instance of this, it may be mentioned that during our stay here a cable car was "held up" in Broadway early one afternoon by an armed gang, and the passengers relieved of their valuables.

It cannot be said that we were much importuned by Mr. Daly's hospitality during our stay in New York. Some of the regulations posted up in the dressing-rooms of his theatre afforded much amusement. Of course they applied to members of his own company only. No member, for instance, was to be seen parading Broadway during certain hours of the afternoon. No tobacco in any form or shape was to cross the threshold of the stage door. Fortunately, however, our pockets were not searched. And perhaps the most amusing rule of all was to

From a Photo by Morrison.

MISS BLANCHE MASSEY.

the effect that no member of his company was to address Mr. Daly personally without being spoken to first. "Speak when you're spoken to," seems a pretty tall order for a democracy wherein all citizens are equal. The formidable list of fines and penalties was enough to strike terror into the heart of any but an Englishman.

We next had a very successful week at the Harlem Opera House, a handsomely appointed theatre, though none too happy in its orchestra. Here, as already mentioned, Monkhouse was taken ill, and had to be left behind when, at the end of the week, we went on to Boston.

December 14th is the anniversary of George Washington's death, and the American people therefore make it a general holiday. Everybody goes out for the day, which, strange to say, is one of unusual festivity and rejoicing. To us it seemed, if possible, more appalling than our own Easter Monday Bank Holiday. Our chief recollection of this particular date, however, lies in the memory of the noise caused by various penny trumpets dinned into the ears by street urchins, and others of that characteristic species.

Shortly before we left, Harlem was visited by a heavy snowstorm, and we found it had preceded us to Boston. We also found the Boston papers full of a scare that Monkhouse was down with smallpox, and could not get settled without some rather troublous interviews with hotel managers and the press.

A Gaiety Girl, once these difficulties were smoothed away, took on at Boston, and we had every reason to be satisfied with our houses during our entire fortnight there.

There were two changes at this time. Our company was augmented by four ladies sent out by Mr. Edwardes—Miss Kearney, Miss Leighton, Miss Carlton, and Miss Bentley, though the last-named did not stay with us any time. Miss Yorke, who had left England with us, also returned from Boston.

Ryley was the next victim to sickness, his place being taken by Cecil Hope.

Special mention must be made of the band at the Boston theatre, which was one of the best we met with in America.

It was here that we acquired a passion for sleighing, than which, if the snow lies sufficiently thick, there are few sensations more enjoyable. Among the places of interest we visited in the neighbourhood were Charlestown and the Bunker's Hill Monument, Pleasant Point, Bay View, Mount Washington, Cambridge, and the buildings of Harvard University, the Washington elm and statue, Randolph, Auburndale, Brighton, and other surrounding townships.

Of Boston itself, its quaint and pretty streets and generally English appearance, much might be written. It has more of a homelike air than any of the other American cities embraced in our tour; and the various monuments recall episodes in English history, which, if they were not all to the credit of the old country, yet endeared us to this city above all others. Though dreary in such wintry weather, it gave one the impression of being a most delightful place to live in, under other conditions—say in spring and summer. So much cannot be said of some other American cities.

On the morning of December 17, we arrived in Washington, where we were rejoined by Monkhouse, sufficiently himself again to resume at once the rôle of "Dr. Brierly."

Albaugh's Opera House, far from being palatial, was designed on the time-honoured barn pattern. Nor was the impression on first entering improved by the absence of electric light, and the presence of an execrable orchestra. It was, moreover, our particular good fortune to have followed Hagenback's travelling menagerie of performing animals, to whom the theatre had been leased the week before.

The stage door had been slightly altered to suit the requirements of the elephants, so that we found everything very roomy. Monkhouse discovered, to his joy, that his dressing-room had been the quarters of the comic bear ; nor were signs wanting in some of the other rooms of recent occupants of eccentric habits.

Nor shall we soon forget, in connection with this Washington theatre, the senatorial receptions in the stage box ; and the frequent interruptions occasioned by the arrival and departure of distinguished guests were a decided innovation, so far as our previous experiences went. There are some American customs which we have no wish to see introduced at home!

Washington is without a doubt one of America's handsomest cities, and we enjoyed glorious weather during our short stay of six days. Few who have once seen them could forget those handsome public buildings, comprising the Capitol, the House of Representatives, and Supreme Court, the latter with a remarkable whispering gallery. Nor will many bird's-eye views beat that which is to be obtained from the summit of the Monument (500 feet high). Memory also suggests the mention of a most realistic panorama of the fight at Gettysburg, and also of an all-too-excellent supper given by De Wolff Hopper out at Overlook Hill. Of the latter function, however, not much can be recalled. A private omnibus conveyed the remains of a dozen festive men back to the hotel at five next morning!

We reached Brooklyn on the Sunday afternoon, the day before Christmas Eve. Two performances we had to give on Christmas Day; but we made up for hard work during this Brooklyn week by revelry and merriment after the day's work was done. Mr. Edwardes, for instance, cabled that we were to have a supper, and, with his usual generosity, made each member of the company a handsome present as a souvenir of the occasion.

Mr. and Mrs. De Wolff Hopper were

among the guests at this supper; and among
the humorous speeches of the evening we
cannot forget Kaye calling for our national
anthem of—

> O Georgie, Georgie Edwardes,
> You're a good 'un, heart and hand;
> You're a credit to you're calling
> And to all your native land,
>   Etc., etc., etc.,

to which the entire company vociferously
responded. After the tables had been
cleared and moved out of the way, dancing
took place, varied by songs, duets, and
recitations. It was an early hour of the
morning when we sought our respective
couches, but the memory of that enjoyable
evening will long be with us.

At Brooklyn, Miss Fitzgerald left us,
to play in *A Twentieth-Century Girl* in
New York, thereby breaking her contract
with Mr. Edwardes, who was successful in

obtaining an injunction against her. On our last night, Leedham Bantock was taken ill, and had to be left behind. Here Bradfield again came to the rescue, and played the "Judge" during the greater part of our stay in Pittsburg.

We left Brooklyn early Sunday morning, December 30, taking the ferry to Jersey City, where we caught the 9 o'clock train, *via* Philadelphia, Harrisburg, and Altoona.

We were journeying towards the setting sun now in good earnest.

Pittsburg to 'Frisco

Pittsburg to 'Frisco

CONSTANT stoppages for hot box made
us fully three hours late, so that it was
something after midnight when we arrived
at Pittsburg. This was one of our most
delightful experiences. There was neither
porter nor cab within hail, so we had to
"hump our own swags," as our Australian
friends would say in their forcible dialect, and
slide over the snow to any quarters that

49

came handy. In this wise we gained a few hours' experience of second-rate American hotels. The experience was not a happy one.

Our first performance, New Year's Eve, at the Duquesne Opera House, was a great success, though the less said about the condition of that establishment behind the scenes the better. We gave two performances on New Year's Day, after which we were rejoined by Leedham Bantock.

Pittsburg, which possesses much of the rural beauty of Bilston, would present an interesting *ensemble* if one could but see it from anywhere. The Duquesne Heights would afford an admirable bird's-eye view but for the all - pervading smoke. At Pittsburg you learn what smoke really is, and the smoke of Tophet would be a veil of gossamer transparency to it. Occasionally, when a kind wind lifts this bandage, you may get glimpses of the grand rivers that wind about the town,—the broad Ohio, the Monongahela, and Alleghany,—all of which were then ice-bound. Particularly striking was the scenery along the Monongahela as far as Cochrane.

After a stay of one week, which many found ample, we left for St. Louis, which was reached Monday morning, January 7, 1895; and here again was an agreeable city. Pittsburg could scarcely come under that category. The "Olympic" was clean, and its orchestra, numbering sixteen, might have been much worse; while with our audiences we had, as regards both numbers and appreciation, every reason to be satisfied. Those who stayed at the Southern Hotel spoke highly of its arrangements. We were most unfortunate in our weather there, and had to console ourselves indoors with the famous Anheuser brew.

Chicago, our next stopping - place, we reached Monday, January 14. The Opera House is a fine building, inside and out, and its band was unquestionably the best we came across in America.

Like 'Frisco, this is a city of hotels. Our first venture was the Auditorium; but we subsequently found that the Victoria Hotel, also facing Lake Michigan, suited us better in every way. Here we had to perform on Sundays as well; but we did not mind this, as *A Gaiety Girl* soon became a general favourite, and during the next three weeks half Chicago came to see it.

Chicago is far from being a pretty city: the lake, which might have beautified it, is hidden from the chief streets by a hideous railway. Indeed, shut in as the place is by water, it

From a Photo by Tal bma.] "A GAIETY GIRL" COMPANY.

gives less suggestion of expansion in the near future than perhaps any of the other American cities which we visited.

In spite of terrible weather, we renewed the pastime of sleighing here, and made some interesting trips in this way. The weather was the worst we experienced during our entire tour. The cold was so intense that the thermometer averaged fourteen degrees below zero, and most of us took to furs and wolf-skin coats. As an example of the excessive rigour of this winter, the lake was frozen over as far as the eye could reach, and a steamer was lost in the ice. During a blizzard that raged for hours with terrific force, the snow found its way inside the window panes, one of which was carried from a shop front and round the corner, where it took off the leg of an unhappy pedestrian. For the truth of this, which

4   53

savours of an American yarn, Monkhouse will vouch.

On Monday, February 4, we left for Milwaukee, where we had a busy week at the Davidson Opera House, at the close of which we parted from our first American chorus, which was disbanded and returned to New York. They would compare very unfavourably with what we were accustomed to in the old country, and equally so with what we afterwards had to work with in Australia, where the average chorus is really excellent.

Here one member of the company, whose anonymity we wish to preserve, purchased a case of Martell's and Henessey's "Three Star" Brandies for the moderate sum of a dollar a bottle. (A bottle of whisky in America will always cost about $3.50). The dealer, having failed in his business, hoped to realise a little ready money on his stock,

which accounted for the extraordinary re-
duction in the price of spirituous liquors.
Malone and certain envious members of
the company would have it, however, that the
contents of these bottles were undrinkable,
and even now will be heard to aver that
the railway conductor on the 'Frisco line
threatened to jump off the car while in
motion, rather than the more painful alternative of a teaspoonful.   The phlegmatic, yet
not teetotal, redskins are said to have hidden
their faces in grief when the bottle was held
up at the car window to their astonished
gaze.   With all these obstacles, however,
the case and the greater number of the
bottles—thanks to the reported questionable
character of the spirits—arrived safely in
'Frisco, and were duly conveyed on board
the *Mariposa*, for medicinal purposes during
the voyage across the Pacific.   An attempt

was made to smuggle a bottle on shore at Samoa, for bartering with the natives; but the owner was informed of the penalty attaching to such contraband, in the shape of an enforced residence on the island for a few months, which, however many the attractions, had not been included in his programme. He therefore wisely refrained, the more so as he was assured on good authority that its only value among the lissom islanders was as an antidote for snake-bite. It was therefore presented to the crew, and we learn that not a single living rat has been seen on the *Mariposa* since. *Revenons à nos moutons.*

Milwaukee was the last place visited by us under Mr. Daly's management.

It is an essentially German city, even the chief newspaper being published in that language. Its public buildings are far from imposing; indeed only one block, a furniture repository or something in that line, struck us as at all remarkable.

As might be expected, beer is the staple drink and brewing the staple industry, and many were our pilgrimages to the shrine of Gambrinus.

On the 10th, we entered on the last stage of our American travels, and for the next three days were speeding west, crossing the frozen Missouri near Omaha, and traversing Nebraska, all extremely monotonous in its mantle of snow.

It was during this part of the journey that there occurred a somewhat trying incident, in which some of our members, judging at least by their own account, narrowly escaped drowning. One dark and stormy night the overhead water-tank overflowed into their sleeping-berths, which entailed a change of cars at Cheyenne. We soon reached the summit of the Rockies, where there is a short halt not far from the monument which indicates the importance of the place. As this stood, however, in several feet of snow, we preferred admiring it from a convenient distance. At Laramie, the next stopping-place, we fell in with some Indians, from whom we purchased a number of spears and other curios. The prairies of Wyoming, which may at any other season be beautiful, were an eternal stretch of white, of which the eye soon tired. Utah we traversed by night, emerging next day into the glorious mountain scenery of Nevada, where the snow lay in some places ten feet deep, in consequence of which a plough had to be fixed on the locomotive; and that night we passed through forty miles of snow sheds. No sooner had we crossed the frontier into California than the temperature rose sensibly, while at the same time the landscape underwent a magic transformation, becoming far more English in character.

The snow was gone, and the weary eyes rested gratefully on the green country and quaint, homelike villages.

Oakland was reached at ten o'clock on the morning of February 14th, and here we took our leave of American railways.

In some respects, nay, in many, these are far in advance of anything we have at home, but the sleeping accommodation is singularly faulty, more especially in the lack of a separate dressing compartment for ladies.

At Oakland, which seems to be appropriately named after the prevailing tree, we took the ferry, followed by a flock of gulls, across to San Fransisco, the most glorious city of all, our last home on American soil.

San Francisco

61

San Francisco

Fascination of this City—The Cable Cars—The Bay
—Defences—Seal Rocks—University—Cemetery
—Slums—Chinatown—Sir Edwin Arnold's un-
due severity — Treatment of Chinese — Their
Theatres—Joss-house—Shakespearian Plays—
We leave 'Frisco—Reflections on America.

A REMARKABLE fascination the city
of St. Francis had for most of us,
though it would be hard to say offhand
wherein lay its particular charm. At anyrate, not all the hospitality of Australian
folks, added to the glories of an Australian
winter, did much to efface the regret with
which we left the Golden Gates. Our first
parents, driven forth from the gates of Para-

dise, could not well have been more crest-
fallen, nor certainly did their pockets contain
much less.

On the 18th we opened at the Baldwin
Theatre, and drew good houses for the next
three weeks.

Here Miss Hobson fell ill, and Miss
Lloyd played "Lady Virginia" during the
greater part of our stay.

It is not our intention to give any lengthy
account of this city of hotels.

The crack hotel, by the way, is the
Palace; but we found the Baldwin quite
comfortable and comparatively moderate in
its tariff.

Riding on a cable car, as understood here,
is a delightful way of getting about; yet as
the cabs are ridiculously expensive, these
cars get crowded to a most uncomfortable
extent. As in Melbourne, the pleasures of

this locomotion are much enhanced by the lofty hills on which the city has been built.

A good view of the bay may be had from the heights on the north side of the Golden Gates. This excellent anchorage affords complete shelter from the great Pacific rollers without; but its defences against invaders of another description strike the visitor as very elementary, which, when we consider its present and future commercial importance, is remarkable. We also took an excursion around the bay in a steam launch, visiting Angel Island, and taking the cable car back from Presidio—a very pleasant outing.

One of the sights of the place—one of the sights, indeed, of the world—are the Seal Rocks, where, within a couple of hundred yards of the cliffs, are the lazy sea lions, indulging in ponderous gambols, and shaking the spray from their sleek coats.

The American Government has, in its wisdom, taken them under its protection; and they seem to know it too, for they betray little alarm at the sight of a passing vessel.

The Golden Gate Park is another favourite resort, and really beautiful; as, at anyrate, one of our party thought, after he had all but trodden on a venomous snake on one of its pathways.

The 'Frisco Cemetery is also one of the most beautiful in a land not perhaps noted for the beauty of its graveyards. Of its thoroughfares, Market Street was un-doubtedly the busiest and most imposing, thronged at all times with a strange medley of humanity, even unto Chinese women and their toddling hopefuls, tricked out in bright-coloured frocks. Like every other city, 'Frisco is not without its slums, near which lay the theatre. Some few establishments there may have been that would have attracted the attention of certain reformers of either sex who have a keen scent for such garbage—dwellings on the doors of which the simple legend "Walk in" took the place of the more respectable professional brass plate. On these, however, we can venture no opinion, for, priding ourselves on our British fortitude and grim respectability, we invariably hastened past those latticed windows, from behind which languishing eyes may have glanced beseechingly but in vain after our retreating forms. Still, he "who runs may read"!

But the most powerful magnet of all, the centre of attraction for all visitors, was fascinating, ruinous Chinatown. Dawdling through its crazy streets, which somehow looked perpetually *en fête*, was our greatest delight, and, alas! its seductive curio stores claimed our last cent. Strangely carved walking-sticks, silk handkerchiefs and sashes of gayest hue, elaborate water-pipes, perfumed joss-sticks, massive ivory chess-men, jars of preserved ginger—these and other temptations were more than Western philosophy could resist. What wonder, then, that scarcely a day elapsed without our visiting these enchanting bazaars and bearing away some fresh trophy!

To Sir Edwin Arnold's fascinating work, *Seas and Lands*, we are grateful, for it relieved the monotony of many a long hour on the Pacific. But in his condemnation of Chinatown we cannot join him; and it seems just possible that the brilliant writer's avowed admiration for everything Japanese may have biassed him in judging the Chow. We visited Chinatown at all hours of the day and night; we haunted its bazaars, restaurants, theatres, and joss - houses—yet

MISS GRACE PALOTTA.

the first we saw of its filthy condition was in his book.

True, "John" has his own ideas on the subject of cleanliness, as indeed on most others; true, his ways are not our ways, and he and his kind may find a comfort not understood by us in getting stupefied with opium, and herding for the night like guinea-pigs, the greatest possible number in the smallest possible space.

This is all very different from our notions of the proper ordering of things; but were the author anyone less eminent than Sir Edwin Arnold, we should be inclined to criticise as nonsense the dictum that Chinatown is "an unmitigated nuisance to the Californian capital, and a perpetual danger to its health and peace."

It would of course have been by far the simpler and safer course to agree with so great an authority on these questions, but conscience cries aloud in vindication of Chinatown; and, after all, *de gustibus*, etc.; to our minds its picturesqueness, like that of the French court of a bygone century, robbed the vice of half its unpleasantness. The quotation is inaccurate, but near enough for practical purposes.

And we will go a step further. Not only do we not, like Sir Edwin Arnold, find subject for wonder in the forbearance exercised by Americans towards their pigtailed brethren, but we have, on the contrary, oftentimes been greatly disgusted at seeing the lazy " hoodlum," or the still more brutal " larrikin," of Australia hustle and kick these hard-working aliens as they dare not hustle and kick their dogs.

Besides the bazaars, the Chinese quarter has more than one restaurant at which the

Western palate may be tickled with the fancy dishes of the Celestial cuisine. In their theatres you may see an interminable performance, in which no women take part; and "foreign devils" are usually accorded seats on the platform.

The "joss-house" is another sight, the sacred joss sitting amid a bodyguard of dolls, with a plate in front for offerings from such of the faithful as may desire to chin-chin his holiness.

Compared with the San Francisco Chinatown, the Chinese quarters of Australian cities are nowhere. The races also proved a great attraction during our stay in 'Frisco.

Mention has been made here and there of various theatrical *matinées* which we were able to visit, and it seemed strange at this end of all things to see Frederick Warde in three Shakespearian plays in the course of two days. At length our stay in this beautiful city came to an end, and we had to leave the Queen of the Pacific on the 8th of March, and the Cliff House faded from view the same afternoon.

Our impressions of America are vivid and varied, though we cannot be expected to do them justice in such a short sketch as this. In fact, we find it difficult to present the reader with a general opinion, since each individual will, in all probability, see the same thing in a different light. Let it then be understood that we are offering but one opinion, and this would probably be modified by a further acquaintance with the country. Humanity is ever a subject of interest, and the American people are not wanting in this respect. We met many very charming Americans of both sexes, and cannot accuse them of any lack of good-fellowship and hospitality. The ladies, however, seem to rule with an arbitrary power over the milder members of the opposite sex, and it will evidently be found that the *New Woman* was born under the " Stars and Stripes." She has certainly the lead in the way of fashion, and our own womenfolk apparently look up to her as to one with authority. The men are a genial, cordial set ; and if the fit of their clothes is not all that could be desired, the tailor and not the unfortunate wearer is at fault, the latter merely contributing a trifle of £8 for his sylish misfit. You can distinguish an Englishman on Broadway at once by the cut of his clothes.

The Yankees, however, are a go-ahead race, and have little time for such a paltry consideration as dress. Indeed, it is highly probable that, but for certain arbitrary police regulations, they would hurry out to business without clothes of any description, and devote the extra five minutes at the shrine of the Almighty Dollar. This is earned easily in America, but unfortunately is just as easily spent. A cab cannot be hired under a dollar, and the economic actor shudders at the idea of having to pay five shillings for a luxury that at home only costs him two. The boot-black charges ten cents for a polish. This is a necessity to which we are forced to accommodate ourselves. You cannot with any degree of safety leave your boots outside your bed-room door, to be cleaned by the early morning, as is the custom in our English hotels. They will disappear, and the hotel proprietor disclaims any responsibility in the matter. You must put on dirty boots in the morning, and trust to find a vacant chair at one of the street corners, from which vantage you may scan with a placid expression the passers-by, who will affect not to notice you. Again, the unwary stranger will grieve much over the expense that it will cost him dining *à la carte* at a restaurant. If he is wise he will eat on the American plan, as it is called, and will thereby save his pocket at the expense of his digestion. On the other hand, he may rejoice in the prodigality of the hotel bars, which provide a free lunch on purchase of a five cent glass of lager beer. This is no doubt a clever enticement and incentive to drink. With five cents in his purse, the fortunate tramp need not starve. He buys a glass of lager, and, in consideration thereof, is permitted to satisfy his hunger as well. Hot sausages, German sausages, Boston beans, American hash, salads and cheese form the chief items of this sumptuous repast. Woodhouse, *alias* Woody, *alias* Wood - O, is of opinion that this is a grand institution, that

would pay well to introduce into this country ;
and we quite agree with him. We may
remark that the Australian hotels have already
borrowed the idea. Now that we are on the
subject of hotels, a few words may be permitted us concerning these palatial buildings
in America. The chief edifice of a Western
city is usually found to be an hotel. It is the
most imposing structure in the place, beside
which the Government houses dwindle to
nothing. As a rule, these hotels are exceedingly comfortable, and we venture the opinion
that the Victoria Hotel at Chicago will stand
second to none. The chief object of interest
about the American hotel lies in its heating
apparatus. It is steam-heat everywhere, and,
to those of us who were unaccustomed to its
vagaries, most uninviting. Even the railway
cars inflict a temporary baking upon their
luckless inmates ; and the passenger escapes

into an atmosphere outside of $-14°$ F. with a sigh of relief.

The overhead railways of New York and Chicago compare favourably with our own underground in way of comfort, and are a decided ornamental improvement in the architectural displays of these cities. In place of the unwieldy omnibus, which is a perpetual eyesore to the traveller in London, the American furnishes us with the elegant and commodious cable car. He has every reason to be proud of so excellent a system. The cars follow one another in rapid succession, and, as it would seem, at a risk of imminent collision. Our one objection lies in the over-crowding. It is easy enough to get on, and you are permitted to find room anywhere you can, even if it be on somebody's lap ; but how some people ever manage to get out again is a mystery, which we will leave our readers to solve. The gripman is an important personage of grim respectability; and if the cable does occasionally break, it is owing to a fault in the machinery. The conductor occupies quite a secondary position. He takes your five cents, and, if you desire it, will hand you a free transfer to any line, so that you may travel about all day for the one fare. Who would not avail himself of such liberality! A word must be said here in favour of the American Express service. When travelling, you are not expected to take any luggage with you except what you may immediately require. Say you wish to undertake the three days' journey by rail from Chicago to 'Frisco. You hand over all your boxes to an attendant at the Express office in Chicago, telling him at what hotel you will stay in 'Frisco. He then hands you a metal ticket, with a number inscribed upon it, and informs you, at the same time, that you will find your luggage awaiting you at the hotel on your arrival, or soon after. You are lucky if you receive it within a week.

Politics present a topic of absorbing interest for all classes in America. We carried away with us some confused ideas of Democracy, Republicanism, Socialism, and Tammany Hall; but do not intend to bewilder the reader by setting forth their essential differences. There seems to be a lot of talk and corruption in the official circles; but as a rule the public are kept pretty well informed. While we were in New York the police were having a warm time of it with the Lexow Committee, and the published revelations of each day added somewhat to the discredit of the force. Dr. Parkhurst, the ecclesiastic reformer, created some excitement by the vigour of his action in purifying the morals of the great Eastern city. He denounced from the platform and the pulpit, and his personal appearance soon became a popular figure for caricature on the boards of the music halls.

Who has not heard of the wonders and mysteries of a Dime Museum? And who, having once bought his experience, would ever enter one again? This is a typical American show. We have seen something like it in an English travelling provincial fair. Imagine a gloomy-looking building, decked on the outside with dummy figures of gaudy appearance, and billed all over with flaring posters of the present attractions. Pay your ten cents and enter ; but, before-hand, take the precaution of buying a large packet of Keatings' Powder, and saturate your handkerchief with the best *eau de Cologne.* We will not attempt a description

of the horrors which will meet your astonished gaze, but will briefly refer to one
incident, which, although harrowing in its
advertised details, proved harmless enough
in the actual deed. A badly executed illustration, at the door of one of the principal
Dime Museums in Chicago, depicted, with an
unsparing use of vermilion, the anatomical dis-
section of a live human being upon a marble
slab. Two legs had already been sawn off,
and the operator was in the act of decapitat-
ing his unfortunate subject. It was intimated
that the public would be admitted to this
exhibition on payment of an extra five cents.
You always have to pay extra to witness
any of the advertised attractions. A morbid
curiosity drew one member of our party,
scientifically inclined, to be present on one
of these gruesome occasions. He was
doomed to disappointment, and, at a later

hour of the day, he indignantly informed us that it was the old pantomime trick of the clown mending the piecemeal body of the policeman, whom he had previously blown from the cannon's mouth. A human-faced chicken proved, on another visit, to be nothing more than the painful exhibition of a half-starved fowl with its beak sawn off. We will not prolong the description of such atrocities. The Americans are great theatre-goers, but above all they love their music halls. There they may gaze with an artistic eye at the presentment of Tableaux-Vivants which would quite shock our prurient-minded British matron by their vivid realism and close imitation of nature. They show great partiality for such subjects as " Venus and Tannhäuser," " Sirens," " After the Bath," " Love and Innocence," " Eve," etc. etc.

The German element exercises a wide-spread influence in all musical affairs, though not always with happy effect; and the English musician who tries his luck in the New World receives but scant encouragement from his Teutonic brethren. There seems to exist a total want of sympathy among all classes of executant musicians, and this necessarily spells misfortune for the luckless members of the weaker minority. Musical Unions are rife all over the country, and have already become a formidable autocratic power. The executive *clique* naturally enough favour the pretensions of their own countrymen, to the exclusion of ofttimes more deserving foreigners. This is particularly the case in New York, Brooklyn, Chicago, Milwaukee and 'Frisco! The conductor of a local theatre is permitted but little authority over the band, which is selected for him by the Union, and he is placed in the unenviable position of having to entreat rather than to command. We have already spoken of our American chorus.

As may be imagined, in spite of our wish to see the colonies, we deeply regretted leaving America. Our stay had been a pleasant one, and the success of *A Gaiety Girl* in ten different cities had been uninterrupted during twice as many weeks. We had met with nothing but kindness, so that our memories of it are bright indeed.

As a place of residence, the average American city is admirable—for Americans. Europeans will, on the whole, prefer a temporary stay only. They will find many things far in advance of what they are used to at home, and a few decidedly behindhand.

One thing struck us, which must in all

MISS DECIMA MOORE.

truth be recorded here, and that was the comparative scarcity of the American beauty of whom we had heard so much.

Many pretty women there certainly were. They occur in most cities. But the fashionable women of Broadway would not bear comparison with those of Regent Street, or Collins Street, Melbourne. Their manners, moreover, are loud, and their dress decidedly *outré*.

Still, America is a grand country from any point of view. Living may be somewhat costly, but at anyrate you do *live*.

The Pacific

87

The Pacific

W HO gave this ocean the name by which
it is commonly known, we do not
happen to remember. "All men are liars,"
as the hasty David once remarked ; and it
may not improbably have suited this ancient
mariner to tempt further filibustering royal-
ties or companies, by depicting this part of
the globe as favourably as possible. Far
from land, it certainly behaves better than
some other oceans ; but along the coasts of

America and Australasia, its mood is generally the reverse of peaceful.

On the day we steamed out of the Golden Gates it was emphatically so; and the name of our ship, the *Mariposa*, added insult to injury, for repose of either body or mind was out of the question. And we had it more or less rough the whole way to the Sandwich Islands, at which we called exactly a week after leaving 'Frisco.

Honolulu, which lies on the island of Oahu, beneath the towering form of the whilom fiery Pouwaina, is a beautiful town, its Chinese quarter picturesque, its European hotels and streets laid out on the most modern scale. We had to make the most of our few hours ashore; so some went up to the extinct crater, others drove to Waikiki Bay, while yet a third party was organised to visit Pali, from the summit of which rock unfortunate prisoners and other offenders were formerly hurled into the sea. This Tarpeian Rock of the South Sea Islands was pronounced extremely picturesque, though on the day we were there a squall played pranks with some of the party. At six in the evening we had to leave this delightful island; and the native band, under the conductorship of Professor Berger, came down to the quay and treated us to an admirable selection from *A Gaiety Girl*, followed by "Auld Lang Syne" and the National Anthem.

Where is civilisation going to stay its hand?

Here we took on board several passengers who had taken a prominent part in the late rising, and were now doomed to exile in consequence of its failure. Thinking to better their condition by restoring the deposed queen, the conspirators met in a hut standing upon a high hill, stored their ammunition, and made everything ready for striking the final blow. Unfortunately, just before the climax, a whisky bottle also attended the meetings, and one dark night the republican police had easy work of it. Still, they proved a harmless lot enough. One noted desperado was usually nursing his youngest child, another played an excellent hand at poker; while a third, surnamed by us "the rebel chief," harangued the second - class passengers daily on the duties of capital, and acquired considerable prestige until we left Apia, where he was hauled aboard in a helpless condition, and the contents of his pockets fell into the sea. At Honolulu we left Professor Lennard, a thought - reader, whose entertainments had afforded some little diversion on the trip.

THE PACIFIC

After this, the Pacific seemed to realise its responsibilities, and we enjoyed over a week of calm weather, the chief incidents of which were crossing the Equator on the 19th, and our visit to Samoa four days later.

On the former occasion, the usual frolics were indulged in.

Neptune came aboard in the person of Harry Monkhouse, who, being conducted to his throne, held forth as follows : — "We understand that our good friend Captain Hayward has on board many strangers to our kingdom, who, beyond feeding our fishes, have never paid tribute. We therefore command that they shall pay toll, or go through the ceremony of introduction to our court. The Chief of Police, 'Rakish Ryley,' will collect the dues."

The roll-call was then read; and as it contained a number of allusions of a very personal nature, it may perhaps be omitted.

There was a good deal of amusement, especially when several of the men were shaved and ducked. It is worthy of re-mark that the gulls and boobies, which had followed us in such numbers from 'Frisco, disappeared entirely after we left Honolulu, nor did we again fall in with any between here and Auckland. It was somewhere near Honolulu, too, that we first saw the beautiful little flying-fish.

On the 23rd, we landed at Apia, island of Upolu, Samoa, and had but a few hours ashore at this beautiful place.

Some of the party, taking guides, made for the villages inland, where they purchased curios of the lissom, mild-eyed lotus-eaters, and sipped the milk of the cocoanut, and one of us even had the good fortune to encounter a native girl named Fasia, who entreated him to marry her offhand. Mrs. Grundy should take a country house on Upolu : she would find plenty of occupation !

For instance, Malone, on the occasion of his visit to the King's Palace, a homely wooden hut, saw a woman cleaning the makeshift of a window, and a little child playing near. In answer to Malone's inquiries, she said that the child was one of King Maliétoa's sons, and added that it was also hers. "Then," said Malone, who is remarkably innocent of the world's ways, "you are the queen." But she explained that she was not that dignified personage ; whereat Malone gave that princeling a handful of coppers, which were eagerly accepted, and went his way, reflecting sadly on the frailty of human nature.

Apia is a lovely place indeed, and who

can wonder at the late R. L. Stevenson selecting it for his home! The tropical vegetation, the picturesque huts among the cocoanut palms at the edge of the sea, the handsome girls and dignified men, were a joy to behold. The only eyesore was the wreck of the German warship *Olga*.

The sea continued calm for two days after Samoa had faded from sight; and on the 25th we had some excellent sports, in which the following came off winners, taking prizes that had been purchased at Apia :—

LADIES' SPORTS.

1. Chalking Pig's Eye . Miss CROSSLAND (strung beads) and Miss LEIGHTON (fan).
2. Potato Race . . Miss MOORE (catamaran) and Miss KEARNEY (tapa).
3. Tug of War . . Miss LLOYD (bangles).
4. Flat Race . . . . Miss KEARNEY (mat) and Mrs. HIBBERT (tapa).
5 Threading the Needle Miss MOORE (tapa) and Mrs. HIBBERT (beads).
6. Egg and Spoon . . Miss CROSSLAND (mat) and Miss KEARNEY (beads).

7. Consolation Prizes . . Miss LUCAS (club), Miss
   ELLIOTT (bangles), Miss
   CARLTON (fan), and Mrs.
   BRADFIELD (fan).

MEN'S SPORTS.

1. Potato Race . . . . GIBSON (club) and MILLS
   (arrow).
2. Chalking Pig's Eye. . KATANAKIS (native dress).
3. Three-legged Race. . GIBSON and CRAIG (arrows).
4. Tug of War . . . . MILLS (cigars).
5. Flat Race . . . . . C. HOPE (catamaran) and
   BRADFIELD (fan).
6. Far-reaching . . . . BRADFIELD (club).
7. Cock-fighting . . . . MILLS (bow and arrow).
8. Hop, Skip, and Jump . CRAIG (club).
9. Jockey Race . . . . MALONE and KATANAKIS
   (arrows).
10. Cigarette Race . . . MALONE (spear) and Miss
    PALOTTA (tapa).
11. Obstacle Race . . . GIBSON (photo).

We just got the sports over in time, for
the sea got abominably rough again next
day, by way of announcing that we were
nearing New Zealand.

The Wednesday was neither rough nor
calm, wet nor fine. In fact, there was no

Wednesday. We had to lose one day at the 180th parallel, and instinct suggested our making it a *matinée* day! In the same spirit, it is not improbable that the old Spanish navigators preferred to lose a Friday or two. Fasting was not much in their line.

Well, we had no 27th of March, but we had a 28th that made up for lost time, for it was very rough and very wet.

We should have mentioned that at Samoa we took on board, as passenger for Sydney, the mother of the late Robert Louis Stevenson, and very charming company she was too, gifted with a quiet humour that was irresistible.

On the Friday (29th March) we touched at Auckland, and had lunch at the Grand Hotel with Mr. Musgrove. We here wit·nessed the performance of *La Cigale* at the Opera House, and re-embarked at midnight, keeping the bold shores of North Island in sight all the next day.

On the third of April, after several days of lovely weather, an unusual luxury in this part of the Pacific, and followed almost to the Heads by a number of albatrosses and Molly Hawks, we entered Port Jackson and admired the renowned harbour.

We only stayed a few hours in Sydney on this occasion, lunching with Mr. Williamson at the "Australia," the largest hotel in the colonies, and catching the afternoon train to Melbourne. Ryley, who had regaled us while in America with a selection of yarns based on a former visit to Australia, came in for some criticism on this journey. We were to have seen old-man-kangaroos gazing unmoved at the passing train, and giant carpet snakes festooned about the telegraph posts : whereas our ideas of wayside scenery along the track were soon limited to miles of ring-barked gums, and unpicturesque hamlets roofed with corrugated iron. The only novel sight, indeed, was an occasional flock of parrots disturbed by the train.

The old *Mariposa* soon returned to 'Frisco, whither we would gladly have accompanied her. For we had scarcely as yet tasted of Australian hospitality.

MISS MAUD HOBSON.

Australia

Australia

I. Melbourne

R EHEARSALS with our new chorus at
the Princess' Theatre, Melbourne,
took up the greater part of the next ten
days, and indeed we had no sooner given

our first performance of *A Gaiety Girl* than we commenced rehearsing *In Town*. This meant continuous hard work and little sight-seeing; and except that some of us saw *The New Boy* at one of the theatres, and others, of more serious tastes, went to hear Borchgrevink lecture on Antarctic Research, our first visit to Melbourne embraced the two least enjoyable months of the whole trip.

IN TOWN.

By Adrian Ross and J. T. Tanner.

Music by F. Osmond Carr.

—— CAST ——

Captain Arthur Coddington }	(A Man about Town)	{ Mr. W. Louis Bradfield
Duke of Muffshire .	. . .	Mr. Charles Ryley
Lord Clanside .	. (His Son)	Miss Florence Lloyd

AUSTRALIA

Rev. Samuel ⎫
Hopkins ⎭ . . (His Chaplain) . ⎰ Mr. LEEDHAM
⎱ BANTOCK

Hoffman . ⎰ (Hall Porter at the ⎱ Mr. FRITZ RIMMA
⎱ "Caravanserai" Hotel) ⎰

Benoli . ⎰ (Manager of the ⎱ Mr. ARTHUR HOPE
⎱ "Caravanserai" Hotel) ⎰

Housekeeper . . . . Miss ETHEL CARLTON

Shrimp . (Call-Boy at the "Ambiguity") Mr. FRED KAYE

Bloggins . (A Solicitor's Clerk) Mr. E. G. WOODHOUSE

The Duchess of Muffshire . Mrs. EDMUND PHELPS

Lady Gwendoline ⎫
Kincaddie ⎭ (Her Daughter) ⎰ Miss BLANCHE
⎱ MASSEY

Marie Belleville . . . Miss GRACE PALOTTA

Flo Fanshawe ⎰ (Principal Dancer at the ⎱ Miss MADGE
⎱ "Ambiguity") ⎰ ROSSELL

Maud ⎰ (Principal Boy at the ⎱ Miss MAUD
Montressor ⎱ "Ambiguity") ⎰ HOBSON

Lottie ⎤
Clara ⎥
⎬ "Ambiguity" Girls
Lillie ⎥
Minnie ⎦

Miss LAURA KEARNEY
Miss CLAIRE LEIGHTON
Miss SOPHIE ELLIOTT
Miss ETHEL SELWYN

—— AND ——

Kitty Hetherton ⎰ (Prima Donna at the ⎱ Miss DECIMA
⎱ "Ambiguity") ⎰ MOORE.

Waiters, Chambermaids, Burlesque Actors and Actresses, etc.

105

ROUND THE WORLD

THE SHOP GIRL.

The Cast of "THE SHOP GIRL" will comprise the
full strength of

MR. GEORGE EDWARDES' COMPANY,

Including Mr. HARRY MONKHOUSE,

Who will reappear in the character of "Mr. HOOLEY."

Mr. Hooley .	(Proprietor of the Royal Stores)	Mr. HARRY MONKHOUSE
Charles Appleby .	(A Medical Student) .	Mr. W. LOUIS BRADFIELD
Bertie Boyd (One of the Boys)		Mr. LEEDHAM BANTOCK
John Brown (A Millionaire)		Mr. CHARLES RYLEY
Sir George Appleby (A Solicitor) .		Mr. CECIL HOPE
Col. Singleton (Retired)		Mr. ARTHUR HOPE
Count St. Vaurien .	(Secretary to Mr. Brown) .	Mr. E. G. COGHLAN
Mr. Tweets .	(Financial Secretary to Lady Appleby)	Mr. E. G. WOODHOUSE
Mr. Miggles .	(Shop-walker at the Royal Stores)	Mr. FRED KAYE
Lady Dodo Singleton	(Charlie's Cousin) .	Miss GRACE PALOTTA
Miss Robinson .	(Fitter at the Royal Stores)	Miss MADGE ROSSELL
Lady Appleby (Charlie's Mother)		Mrs. EDMUND PHELPS
Ada Smith . .	(An Apprentice at the Royal Stores)	Miss MAUD HOBSON
Faith . Hope . Charity .	Lady Appleby's Daughters	Miss ETHEL SELWYN Miss LAURA KEARNEY Miss SOPHIE ELLIOTT

Maud Plantagenet⎫   Of the   ⎧Miss Blanche Massey
Eva Tudor .   ⎪   ⎪Miss Florence Lloyd
             ⎬ Syndicate ⎨
Lillie Stuart .   ⎪ Theatre   ⎪Miss Ethel Carlton
Maggie Jocelyn   ⎭   ⎩Miss Claire Leighton
Bessie Brent ("The Shop Girl") Miss Decima Moore

ACT 1. . . . . THE ROYAL STORES.
ACT 2. . FANCY BAZAAR AT KENSINGTON.
Quaint Japanese Song and Dance,
Miss Madge Rossell and Mr. Fred Kaye.
Pierrot Dance,
Mdlles. Maggie Crossland, Lucy Murray, May
Lucas, and Madge Rossell.

Indeed, it was not until our last week, when we were staging our third piece, *The Shop Girl*, that some excitement was furnished on the day of the Theatrical Carnival, 29th May, which was held in the Exhibition Buildings.

The crowd was enormous, and the fund in aid of which the Carnival had been organised benefited considerably; while the directors presented each and all who took part in it with a little gold medal, commemorative of the occasion. Bradfield gave a most clever and successful entertainment in a booth of his own ; while in another, Monkhouse and Kaye, assisted by Mrs. Phelps, Miss Leighton, Leedham Bantock, and Fritz Rimma, gave a travesty on *Hamlet* in the Richardson show booth (*Shop Girl*). The refreshment booths were in charge of Miss Hobson and Miss Palotta, assisted by Misses Selwyn, Rossell, Carlton, etc.; while Miss Moore, with Misses Kearney and Elliott, had charge of the booth containing photographs and cut flowers.

There was also a football match in costume, and a successful race table in charge of Miss Lloyd, with Miss Massey and Miss Leighton to assist.

And so, on the 31st May, by special train after the performance, we left for Adelaide.

We had, as already said, been too hard worked at Melbourne to see very much of its surroundings. Fern Tree Gully and Healesville are about the only beauty spots we visited. The city itself was impressive enough; still more so, when one recalls its meteoric rise and fall. The appointments of the Princess' Theatre, in front as behind, are deserving of the highest praise. There is, however, one serious drawback in the number of rats with which it is infested. Boots, grease - paints, powder, and puffs appeared equally acceptable to them, and the ravages they committed on our stage properties were considerable. The orchestra was indeed so excellent—second to none save that at Sydney—that we took a few of the members with us to Adelaide; which did not, however, do much to raise the hopeless mediocrity of the local band. The cable - car system, the best in Australia, reminded us of San Francisco. Shorn of its suburbs, the Victorian capital would be a poor city indeed, though a few of its streets and buildings are grand. Of its hotels, much cannot be said; though many of us were exceedingly comfortable at the Oriental and Grand Coffee Palace. One establishment in Melbourne every visitor must remember, and that is the " Arcade," kept by Cole, the colonial Whiteley. Now that we had no longer the beloved Chinese Quarter to relieve us of spare cash, many were our visits to this universal provider's, who, among other trifles, stocks one million books.

II. Adelaide

We opened at the Theatre Royal, Adelaide, on the night of our arrival, and in ten days we gave all three pieces to crowded houses.

Adelaide strikes you at once as a particularly clean city, besides being, for its size, laid out to better advantage than any other in the colonies. But it is further from the sea than some folks at home seem to imagine, and the journey by rail is anything but a pleasant one. Its public buildings show the usual lavish outlay, and the Museum is as good as any in the country. Unlike Melbourne, too, the surroundings, being hilly, are beautiful, and the excursion to Burnside, with its orange trees and bijou waterfall, was pleasant indeed.

Our stay here was, however, so short that any adequate account of this peaceful little city is impossible.

On Wednesday, the 12th June, we did a day's work at which the Eight Hours party would have stood aghast, for, after giving a *matinée* and evening performance, we left by midnight train for Sydney. There was a couple of hours' halt next day at Melbourne, after which we proceeded, *via* Albury, an uncomfortable journey in badly-appointed cars, and through the dreariest of landscapes.

III. Sydney

At Sydney we spent perhaps the most enjoyable time of the whole tour. This may be in part due to the beautiful weather we enjoyed there. As first experienced at Melbourne, the much-vaunted Australian winter had not impressed us favourably. The mornings were raw, and the evenings worse. But in Sydney, the weather was unexceptionable for three months. A few sultry days there may have been, and two, or at most three, on which wet weather kept us indoors ; but taken all round, the weather was phenomenal.

A word must be said *en passant* for the Empire Hotel, and its attentive hostess, Mrs. Baumann. The *cuisine* was excellent, and our comfort was studied in every way.

An amusing incident may be related here which Kaye tells about an experience he had, from which he would warn all future visitors to Sydney. On the morning after our arrival he was lying snug in bed, not having quite made up his mind whether to get up for his breakfast or not, when a knock at the bedroom door called forth the usual response. A gentlemanly - dressed man walked in, and familiarly saluted Kaye by his Christian name, telling him that he had just been to see Charley Ryley,—who happened to be staying in the same hotel,— and that he had accepted an invitation to dinner on a day the following week, to which he begged that Kaye would do him the

honour of coming. Thinking him an old
acquaintance of Ryley, by the affectionate
manner in which this gentleman spoke of
"Charley," Kaye imagined nothing unusual,
and promised to let him have his reply.
The visitor, however, seemed in no hurry to
go; and after sundry glances about the
room, and various remarks concerning the
depression in business, he made his way to
the dressing-table, on which Kaye had
turned out the contents of his pocket (including money) the preceding night. Picking
up a sovereign with a *nonchalant* air, he
said carelessly, "I suppose you can let me
have this until Monday." "Certainly," replied Kaye, not yet sufficiently awake to
the world's wickedness. "May as well make
it two," was the inviting rejoinder, as the
stranger added another precious gold coin
to his former loan, and gradually made his

way to the door, departing with the friendly
words, "Hope to see you on Monday, and
pay you back without fail." The story does
not end here. Kaye began to smell a rat,
and, jumping out of bed, dressed hurriedly,
and made his way to Ryley's room, from
whom he learned that he had no such friend
as Kaye described. The landlord was next
interrogated as to the man's identity, and,
having received a full description of his
personal appearance, said laconically, "Oh
that's ——. How much money had you on
your dressing-table?" Kaye bethought a
moment, and then said, "About five
pounds." "Then you are three pounds to
the good," replied the landlord; whereat
Kaye dissembled, and departed glad at
heart. He never saw that man again.

As on the previous occasions, we opened
at the Lyceum with *A Gaiety Girl*, June

15th, and the piece ran for three weeks with unbroken success, when it was followed by *In Town*, July 6th. This was still better received. *The Shop Girl* ran from August 3rd, also for three weeks. On August 5th, we started rehearsing a fourth piece, *Gentleman Joe*, then in the course of a long run at home, and which we played for a fortnight only, though it was a great favourite.

The cast was distributed as follows :—

Gentleman Joe (a Hansom Cabman) .	{ Mr. W. LOUIS BRADFIELD
The Earl of Donnybrook . .	Mr. CHARLES RYLEY
Mr. Ralli-Carr	. Mr. CECIL HOPE
Hughie Jaqueson	Mr. ARTHUR HOPE
Mr. Pilkington Jones . .	. Mr. FRED KAYE
William (a Page Boy) . .	. Miss FLORENCE LLOYD
Dawson (a Butler). . .	Mr. LEEDHAM BANTOCK
James (a Footman) . .	. Mr. FRITZ RIMMA
Postman	. Mr. A. ADELT
Policeman	. Mr. W. L. GORDON
Photographer . .	. Mr. E. G. WOODHOUSE
Photographer's Assistant .	. Mr. J. HUNTER
Mrs. Ralli-Carr . . .	. Miss GRACE PALOTTA
The Hon. Mabel Cavanagh .	. Miss BLANCHE MASSEY

W. LOUIS BRADFIELD.

AUSTRALIA

Miss Lalage Potts	Miss MAUD HOBSON
Miss Pilkington Jones . . .	Miss LAURA KEARNEY
Miss Lucy Pilkington Jones . .	Miss MADGE ROSSELL
Miss Amy Pilkington Jones . .	Miss SOPHIE ELLIOTT
Miss Ada Pilkington Jones . .	Miss ETHEL SELWYN
A Cook	. Miss CLAIRE LEIGHTON
Emma (a Maid Servant) . .	Miss DECIMA MOORE

On Wednesday, August 21st, there was
a *matinée* benefit to Monkhouse, who was
returning home a fortnight later.

The programme included—

Overture—"A Gaiety Girl" .	THE LYCEUM ORCHESTRA
Comic Sketch . . .	Messrs. FOREMAN and FANNAN

SELECTIONS FROM SECOND ACT OF

THE SHOP GIRL.

Duet (Japanese) . .	. Mr. KAYE and Miss ROSSELL
Song—"Di Di" . . .	Miss MOORE and CHORUS
Song—"Do not trust him"	Mr. BRADFIELD and CHORUS
Pierrot Dance . .	{ Mdlles. ROSSELL, LUCAS, CROSSLAND, and MURRAY

Serio-Comic Song .	. Miss FLORRIE FORDE
Song	. Miss ADA COLLEY

---

8   117

ROUND THE WORLD

SELECTIONS FROM

A GAIETY GIRL.

Lady Virginia . . . . Miss MAUD HOBSON
Mina (her Maid) . . . . Miss GRACE PALOTTA
Alma Somerset (a "Gaiety" Girl) . Miss BLANCHE MASSEY
Rose Brierly . . . . Miss DECIMA MOORE
Captain Goldfield . . . . Mr. CHARLES RYLEY
Sir Lewis Grey (a Judge) . Mr. LEEDHAM BANTOCK
Dr. Brierly . . . . Mr. HARRY MONKHOUSE

———

Duet—"Dear Papa" Mr. MONKHOUSE and Miss MOORE
Trio . . . . { Miss HOBSON, Mr. BANTOCK, and Mr. MONKHOUSE
Song—"Sunshine above" . . Mr. CHARLES RYLEY
Song— { "When your Pride has had a Tumble" } Miss GRACE PALOTTA

═══

Comic Sketch . . . THE SAKERS (Alfred and Alice)
Song—"Poor Wandering One" Miss FLORENCE ESDAILE

═══

A DRAMATIC INCIDENT IN ONE ACT, ENTITLED

WAITING.

Characters by

Miss MYRA KEMBLE and Mr. HARRY MONKHOUSE.
Delory and Holland.

———

118

AUSTRALIA

PEPITA.

Bombardos	Mr. CHARLES RYLEY
Pataques	Mr. WILLIAM ELTON

Song—"Embarrassment" . . Miss ISABEL WEBSTER

A DRAMA IN ONE ACT, ENTITLED

THE GOLD DIGGERS.

Nat the Roarer (a Digger) . . .	Mr. SCOT INGLIS
Jake Guzzle (Boss of the "Shanty") .	Mr. COUGHLIN
Mulberry Jim (a Poet)	Mr. C. THOMAS
Rich Jim (a Digger) . .	Mr. HARRY MONKHOUSE
Titus Brown (a Nigger) . .	Mr. HARRY LESTON
Nelly Carden (Jim's Wife) . .	Miss MAUD HOBSON
Freddy (their Child)	Little BABY LOHR

Song . . . . Mr. HARRY SHINE

SELECTION FROM FIRST ACT OF

IN TOWN.

Duchess of Muffshire . . .	Mrs. EDMUND PHELPS
Gwendoline Kincaddie ⎱ (her Daughter) ⎰ .	. Miss BLANCHE MASSEY
Mr. Hopkins (a Tutor) . .	Mr. LEEDHAM BANTOCK

Lord Clanside	.	.	.	. Miss FLORENCE LLOYD
Hoffman (Hall Porter)	.	.	.	. Mr. FRITZ RIMMA
Benoli (Hotel Proprietor)	.	.		Mr. ARTHUR HOPE
Bloggins (a Solicitor's Clerk)		.		Mr. E. D. WOODHOUSE
Captain Coddington	.	.		Mr. W. LOUIS BRADFIELD

Duet—" Dear Mamma"   Mrs. PHELPS and Miss MASSEY

Trio—"Taradiddle" . { Messrs. BRADFIELD, BANTOCK, and Miss LLOYD.

Honorary Musical Directors,
Messrs. GRANVILLE BANTOCK and GEO. HALL.

Honorary Stage and Business Managers,
Messrs. GARNER and EMERY.

So much for our work in Sydney. The last fortnight was taken up with second editions of our other pieces ; and on the last night of all we gave a miscellaneous bill, of which more anon.

Sensational as was the rise of Melbourne, and grand even her fall, she is now in the slough of despond, the proud Victorian capital, humbled before her rival. As a city of the chess - board order, Melbourne is remarkable. The public buildings are magnificent; indeed the Parliament House is out and away the finest in the colonies, and the only building worthy of sheltering that august body, the Federated Legislature, which up to the present exists only in the fertile womb of the near future, and holds its sittings in the equally fertile imagination of Sir Henry Parkes.

Melbourne—"Smelbourne," as the insolent *Bulletin* has it—is in the opinion of some the queen of Australian cities; but to our mind Sydney, the more English, more stable city, seemed beyond question destined to be the future capital of Australasia. Its business streets, named after King George of blessed memory and the great Pitt, would not shame any European capital; but no thoroughfare is more characteristically Australian than Macquarie Street.

Here we have Whitehall and Harley Street in one, with a suggestion of Park Lane at midsummer. Along one side of the street run the beautiful Botanic Gardens, of which Sydney folk are so justly proud. If they didn't make their harbour, they can at least claim the gardens, where rocky slopes have been, at great expense, transformed into shady bowers of tropical fernery, winding walks, stately avenues, and ornamental lakes. From the street above, these gardens slope down to the shores of Farm Cove, where the smart squadron lies at anchor off Garden Island, the hospitality of which was extended to some of our party.

Then, in Macquarie Street, besides the residences of all the leading medical men, we find most of the Government buildings —the Treasury, Department of Railways, Public Library, Hospital, Parliament House,

Mint, and Bankruptcy Court. Business at the last-named purgatory is generally brisk, and many Sydney tradesmen amuse themselves by quarterly excursions "up King Street." The Treasury is a fine building, disfigured by the usual moiety of gingerbread ornamentation; the Library is excellent, well ventilated and lighted, and with a collection of over 10,000 books on Australian topics alone.

The Parliament-House is a tumbledown old barn, seen from the outside, though its interior is more pleasing, and the proceedings are occasionally amusing. The Mint is another octogenarian building; but a visit is interesting, on account of the various golds one can see there — gold from Charters-Towers, from Mount Morgan, from the Palmer, and from one or two small New South Wales fields. Over twenty million ounces of gold have been coined here.

Besides these buildings, Macquarie Street must contain quite fifty boarding-houses, at some of which the fare was, however, somewhat ascetic. It was at one of these that the terrible Dacre tragedy occurred. And before quitting this street, we must give it one parting word of praise. It is quite the least dusty in Sydney—by no means a trifle in a city where, for the most part, the dust gets into everything, even the sugar. The Corporation—all honour to them — have a weakness for sprinkling sand over the wood pavements whenever rain threatens. This is done in all kindness to save the horses' knees; but the rain disappoints,—a little way it has in that land, —and the dust gets in the horses' eyes, and makes their drivers expostulate in language the reverse of good taste.

Of Sydney's palatial buildings we will give no account, though they surpass in every respect those of cities of ten times its years.

Fine buildings are a passion with colonials; and each capital wants the biggest thing in public halls. The ratepayers jib at this flagrant jobbery, but they are inordinately proud of it all the same. The visitor likes it better still, for he can admire the sights without having to put his hand in his pocket. The Town Hall is quite the finest in the colonies, and contains the largest organ in the world. Through the courtesy of the Mayor we had an opportunity of hearing M. Wiegand exhibit the capabilities of this excellent instrument with complete command. Here we may add that our kind host, although not a patron of theatres, invited us to inspect his suite of rooms, and therein entertained us in the most hospitable manner. Of striking architecture, the Town Hall would compare favourably with our Mansion House, and is far preferable to the Paris Hôtel de Ville.

The Lands-Office and Post-Office are also magnificent structures; and from the summit of the tower of the latter building you may get a superb view over the harbour, Botany Bay, the Parramatta and Lane Cove Rivers, and the green country inland, away to the Blue Mountains in the background.

But the abuses of the postal arrangements let us try and forget, even though we cannot forgive. Apart from the absurdity of having to pay on a letter for anywhere beyond the confines of the city only one halfpenny less than the cost of sending it to Iceland or Siberia, there are a number of red-tape nuisances that irritate the visitor, although the residents seem to like them. For instance, there is no parcels post to the States! Printed matter and manuscripts are charged at letter

rate, unless addressed to an editor or pub-
lisher. So that the latter functionary, wishing
to return them, has to pay heavily. And
many parcels, on which postage was nominally
paid to the door of the addressee, are left at
the post office, a notification being stuck in
the letter box that, if wanted, they can be
fetched.

These are comparatively dignified means
of getting the maximum of pay for the
minimum of work; but the Department
recently conceived the brilliant notion of
reprinting sheets of obsolete stamps for sale
to the collector. In doing which, it is only
fair to say, it brought down on its head the
ridicule of the press.

To anyone interested in the conduct of
prisons, a visit to the courteous governor of
Darlinghurst, Mr. Herbert, may be recom-
mended. We went over this exceedingly

well-appointed jail on several occasions, each of which confirmed our opinion that colonial prison life is a kind of picnic. In a certain section of both Press and Parliament there is, for reasons into which it is unnecessary to inquire too particularly, a deep-rooted sympathy with offenders of every grade; and the slightest attempt at discipline, even with the most brutalised larrikin, calls forth leading articles in *Truth*, or other papers of that kidney, headed: OUR INHUMAN PRISON SYSTEM.

The inmates are so well fed and cared for that they never make the slightest attempt at escape; and when released, seldom fail, after a brief interval of unprofitable liberty, to renew the treatment.

Among the prison's more distinguished inmates have been " Moonlight," " Thunderbolt," and other gentlemen of the road, *alias* bushrangers, known to fame; and on the beam over the drop are inscribed the names of the desperadoes of both sexes who have paid the last penalty. There is nothing of the sensational about the colonial jails. Executions are not made public by tolling bell or black flag flying in the breeze; and the governor has not even the customary museum of relics with which to charm the morbid.

The University, which can be reached by the cheap and convenient yet dirty steam-tram, has a hall equal for size to anything at Oxford, although it naturally lacks that touch of beauty which only age and associations can bestow. The students include women, and some very attractive undergraduates there are too. *Mens eadem, sidere mutato* is the appropriate motto of this Southern-Cross university; while under the arms of the

Melbourne *alma mater*, younger by three years, is inscribed the more modest legend, *Postera crescam laude*.

Some of the other buildings we visited also, but memory unfortunately fails to recall their attractions. To the Observatory, a great improvement on the older establishment out Parramatta way, we were most hospitably welcomed by Mr. H. C. Russell, the Government Astronomer, who brought us nearer to that disappointing constellation, the Southern Cross, and showed us some of his beautiful sky photographs.

Those who cared about natural history found plenty to interest them in the mammalian and fish collections in the Museum, a substantial building that faces the parched quadrangle styled by courtesy Hyde Park. And with stuffed specimens they must needs be satisfied, since Sydney has no

Aquarium, and its "Zoo"—well, it will be kinder not to describe it.

Of Sydney's amusements, a word. They are varied, as Sydney folks are fond of pleasure. First and foremost came the picnic,—that comfortless *al fresco* repast, con- stantly interrupted by ants and black spiders, bush fires, and snake alarms,—for which Australians have such a passion. For this taste,—craze, rather,—climate is answerable.

The harbour, too, was at the week end one vast playground, and Sydney's citizens pass most of their lives yachting over its vast expanse, or fishing its hundred inlets.

Theatre-parties, too, are another institution, though there were none of those somewhat effusive receptions which interrupted us occasionally in America. Lecturing is sure to pay well in the colonies, if both the lecturer and his subject are good ; but it is a fatal mistake to think that anything is good enough, for the audiences are, on occasion, exceedingly critical. Thus, Mr. Villiers, the war correspondent, drew very full houses during the time he stayed in Sydney; though other lecturers out from home, notably a popular ecclesiastic and an interviewer of some reputation, failed ignominiously.

Before glancing at the picturesqueness of its surroundings, we may mention the chief means of getting about the city itself.

First of all there are the steam-trams, unsightly and noisy arrangements with all the vices of trains and none of their virtues, which run at low fares, without distinction of class, to all parts of the city, and to some outlying suburbs like Botany and Coogee.

Omnibuses there are, too, with wonderful drivers who, unassisted by anything so modern as a conductor, control their horses,

From a Photo. by Sarony.

LEEDHAM BANTOCK.

collect fares, give change, hail passengers, and even regulate the opening and shutting of the door by a footstrap.

Then there is a cable-tram, on the same principle as the Melbourne cars, working along an endless steel rope from a central power station. As a short section of this cost the Government just over £150,000, we should consider it rather a fancy undertaking, especially as the fares are exceedingly low. The hansom is also much in vogue,—the costly and bohemian hansom; but never believe a word of travelled liars' nonsense about the shady morals of those Australians who ride in hansoms. There is nothing that would not equally apply to London or any other capital.

A peep we must give, in conclusion, at a few of the beauty spots in the neighbourhood. Few cities—none, at all events, in

9 133

Australia — are happier in their surroundings.

Well watered is this corner of New South Wales, and on some of the rivers, to say nothing of the harbour and Narrabeen Lakes, there is some lovely scenery. The Lane - Cove River and Hawkesbury are specially beautiful, as also parts of the George's River at Como and Sans Souci. There are peeps in the National Park more exquisite than any glade of the New Forest or Richmond Park, of which so much is made in the old country. At the same time, there is a certain undeniable monotony in the tree-ferns and palms that are the prevailing feature in tropical scenery. But typically Australian above all Sydney's other show - places, are the rugged rockeries near Bulli. Few of us visited the Blue Mountains and the famous

Jenolan Caves, the *pièce de resistance* of the colony; but those who did, brought back wonderful reports of the marvels they had seen.

To the Harbour we cannot attempt to do justice. " We got into Port Jackson early in the afternoon, and had the satisfaction of finding the finest harbour in the world, in which a thousand sail of the line may ride in the most perfect security." Thus wrote Captain Philip in his despatches more than a hundred years ago, and the "finest harbour in the world," notwithstanding the claims of Rio and one or two other candidates for the premiership, it has since remained.

Sydney people are untiring in their praises of this wonderful piece of landlocked scenery, which, on his own confession, baffled even Trollope's pen.

For the tired voyager, who has knocked about for weeks on the open sea, there is a charm almost supernatural in the infinite peace suggested by this vast anchorage, shut in from the ocean and dazzling the eye with its rapid succession of tranquil bays and bluff headlands, some bald and deserted, others clad in every shade of green, and crowned with trim villas of every design. Islands there are to enhance the variety of this lovely lagoon—Garden Island, with its gunboats, Shark Island, Fort Denison (which has the homely sobriquet of Pinchgut, in honour of a prisoner who was once starving there, until his wife heroically braved the sharks and swam across each night with provisions), and others.

Many of the bays, which from the upper deck of a P. & O. look inconsiderable enough, would accommodate whole squadrons. Middle Harbour, the most beautiful arm of Port Jackson, would hide many of the world's navies. Attractive as this harbour must have been a hundred years back, Sydney architects and gardeners have made it infinitely more so ; and there is something reasonable, after all, in the national pride. Potts Point would look bare indeed, and Darling Point deserted, without the pretty dwellings that are mirrored in the still water below.

Some of its bays are lovely—Neutral and Mossman's Bays particularly so. Of a Saturday afternoon, Manly was the favourite rendezvous, and half Sydney boards the cheap, swift steamers, and devours the *Bulletin* and passion - fruit. And down there by the rolling Pacific, the young ones ride ponies, and paddle out of reach of the sharks.

Watson's Bay, on the other side of the harbour, is very different, and the sleepy little hamlet is little visited save by the pilots who live there. There is no beach, as the ocean breaks against the perpendicular cliffs, and resounds in the gap that witnessed the break-up of the *Dunbar* in 1857.

The drive, however, from Sydney along the new South Head road, gives unrivalled views of the harbour; and the Macquarie Lighthouse, which flashes its white beams fifty miles seaward, is well worth inspecting.

Oystering among the rocks is a favourite pastime with the Watson's Bay folks—think of it, ye epicures : going forth with hammer and chisel, and feeding to repletion on rock oysters !

To the harbour we do not pretend to have done justice, having merely jotted down such memories as recur after a lapse of months.

Other features of Sydney would doubtless occur to us if memory were but jogged sufficiently. For instance, there are the two Chinese quarters ; not a patch upon the

'Frisco rookeries, yet sufficiently interesting, doubtless, to those who had not seen the others. The visitor delights in driving bargains, as he is pleased to consider his purchases, in bath-slippers, water-pipes, whist-markers, and other rubbish, while the wily Yellow One ties up the parcels with impassive countenance.

The Arcades, too, found here as in Melbourne, are usually thronged in Sydney; and on Saturday morning the *élite* assemble there, and chatter and ogle, the gentler sex, with those dark eyes they know how to use so well.

Some account might have been given, too, of Sydney's palatial banks and leviathan insurance buildings, two of the latter being somewhat the same size as our Royal Exchange. But Australian banks are a sore subject with some.

Nor must we forget that popular function of Sydney and her rival, the "send off," in which large crowds of friends assemble on the quay, and speed the parting ship with cheers and bouquets. And the professional photographer is perched close by, and transfers to glass their tears and gestures of sorrow.

There were also excursions up the Hawkesbury River, the Rhine of Australia, where, on one occasion, we took part in a wallaby drive, in which the only ingredient wanting was the wallaby. Shooting over foxhounds did not prove a success, and only one small scrub-wallaby paid the penalty. Several times we camped up near Flat Rock, Middle Harbour, until the sameness of that enclosure palled on us. Parramatta and Botany were also favourite excursions.

Lest we should be in danger of accumulating any spare cash afar from the temptations of Chinatown and Cole's Arcade, our good genius furnished a diversion in the shape of Tost & Rohu's curio shop, not far from the post office, and several sales of furs and rugs at Lawson's auction rooms in Pitt Street.

A mania set in, moreover, for buying curious pets. Arthur Hope started a native bear, which died almost immediately in its devoted master's arms. Cecil Hope ran a diminutive and unprepossessing monkey; and others were the proud owners of diamond-snakes, baboons, opossums, and what not. Jamrach himself might have coveted such a collection.

Our last night in Sydney was, as afore-mentioned, devoted to a special mixed pro-gramme, and the reception it met with was phenomenal. Indeed, the house had been crowded the last ten nights in response to short revivals of *In Town, Gentleman Joe*, and *A Gaiety Girl.*

But on 19th September we played to the largest audience of all, the programme being as follows :—

The Second Act of

IN TOWN.
— CAST. —

Capt. Arthur Coddington (a Man about Town) } . Mr. W. Louis Bradfield

Duke of Muffshire . . . . Mr. Charles Ryley

Lord Clanside (his Son) . . Miss Florence Lloyd

Rev. Samuel Hopkins (his Chaplain) Mr. Leedham Bantock

Hoffman (Hall Porter at the "Caravanserai Hotel") } . . Mr. Fritz Rimma

Benoli (Manager of "Caravanserai Hotel") . . . } . Mr. Arthur Hope

Shrimp (Call Boy at the "Ambiguity") Mr. Fred Kaye

Bloggins (a Solicitor's Clerk) . Mr. E. G. Woodhouse

Fritz (a Waiter) . . . . . . Mr. Gates

Housekeeper . . . . Miss Ethel Carlton

Tybalt . . . . Mr. Arthur

The Duchess of Muffshire . . Mrs. Edmund Phelps

Lady Gwendoline Kincaddie (her Daughter) . } Miss Blanche Massey

Marie Bellville . . . . Miss Grace Palotta

AUSTRALIA

Flo Fanshawe (Principal Dancer at the "Ambiguity") . }	Miss MADGE ROSSELL.
Maud Montressor (Principal Boy at the "Ambiguity") . }	Miss MAUD HOBSON

Lottie .		. Miss LAURA KEARNEY
Clara .	"Ambiguity" Girls	. Miss CLARE LEIGHTON
Lillie .		. Miss SOPHIE ELLIOTT
Minnie .		. Miss ETHEL SELWYN

—— AND ——

Kitty Hetherton (Prima Donna at the "Ambiguity") . } . Miss DECIMA MOORE

Waiters, Chambermaids, Burlesque Actors
and Actresses, etc.

—— The *PAS SEUL* by Miss MADGE ROSSELL. ——

The *PAS DE TROIS* by Mdlles.
MAGGIE CROSSLAND, LUCY MURRAY, and MAY LUCAS.

SELECTIONS FROM

THE SHOP GIRL

AND

GENTLEMAN JOE.

1. "The Japanese Dance."	1. "The Coon Dance."
2. "Di Di."	2. "In my 'Ansom."

The Second Act of

A "GAIETY" GIRL.

—— CAST. ——

Charles Goldfield .	Officers	. Mr. CHARLES RYLEY	
Major Barclay .	of	. . Mr. FRED KAYE	
Bobbic Rivers .	the	. . Mr. CECIL HOPE	
Harry Fitz Warren	Life	Mr. E. G. WOODHOUSE	
Ronny Farquhar .	Guards	. Mr. ARTHUR HOPE	

Sir Lewis Gray (Judge of the Divorce Court) .   Mr. LEEDHAM BANTOCK

Lance (Goldfield's Servant) .   . Mr. C. W. BERKELEY

Auguste (Bathing Attendant)   .   Mr. FRITZ RIMMA

Dr. Montague Brierly .   .   . Mr. W. L. BRADFIELD

Rose Brierly (his Daughter)   . Miss DECIMA MOORE

Lady Edytha Aldwyn	Society	Miss LAURA KEARNEY	
Miss Gladys Stourton	Ladies	Miss SOPHIE ELLIOTT	
Hon. Daisy Ormsby .		. Miss ETHEL SELWYN	

Lady Gray (Wife of Sir Lewis)   Mrs. EDMUND PHELPS

Alma Somerset .	Girls	Miss BLANCHE MASSEY	
Cissy Verner .	of	Miss FLORENCE LLOYD	
Haidee Walton	the	Miss CLARE LEIGHTON	
Ethel Hawthorn	"Gaiety"	. Miss MADGE ROSSELL	

Lady Virginia Forrest .   .   . Miss MAUD HOBSON

Mina (Maid to Lady Virginia) .   . Miss GRACE PALOTTA

The *PAS SEUL* by Miss MADGE ROSSELL.

The *CARNIVAL DANCE* by Mesdames
MAGGIE CROSSLAND, LUCY MURRAY, and MAY LUCAS.

That same night we returned to Melbourne, where we played for five weeks at the Princess' Theatre, opening on 21st September with *Gentleman Joe,* and continuing with *The Shop Girl, A Gaiety Girl,* and *In Town;* and on our last night (25th October) repeated the same special programme, which was also given at Bradfield's Benefit on the same afternoon, a function rather poorly attended, as all Melbourne had turned out to do honour to Lord Brassey's landing. Indeed, what with the preparations for its new Governor's reception, and one or two important race meetings, notably the Caulfield Cup, the capital was rather gay during our second stay there. We were not particularly successful in our little ventures at Flemington, so we are unanimous in denouncing horse-racing as the curse of the colonies.

There were one or two unavoidable alterations in the cast of two of the pieces. In *The Shop Girl*, W. Elton took the place of Monkhouse, who, as previously recorded, had gone home ; and the French Count was played by Mr. Berkeley.

In *A Gaiety Girl*, Bradfield appeared in the part of Dr. Brierly.

So, on the 26th of October, we embarked on the Orient Co.'s steamer *Oruba*, leaving behind Miss Moore, who was determined to witness the run for the Melbourne Cup ; Cecil Hope, who was bent on farming in South Africa, as the short cut to health and wealth ; and another member of the company, who had married a Sydney gentleman.

The night before, there had been quite an ovation at the stage door, and Kaye was carried through the streets on six stalwart shoulders. And this afternoon we got a famous "send off," which scarcely consoled us, however, for the rough seas we at once encountered on doubling the Otway.

But to the homeward progress one last chapter by itself.

It seems in place to give first some little idea of our Australian cousins, what sort of communities they form, and wherein their daily life differs from our own. Everyone of course carries away different impressions from such a visit, but much that appears in books about these same colonials has struck us as far wide of the truth.

Visitors to the colonies have, for instance, laid great stress on the absence of what they are pleased to call "society" in those Southern cities. In the first place, it is questionable whether this same society is an unmixed blessing to any community. Indeed,

it may be questioned whether it may not some-
times be an unmixed something else. Whether
this is so, however, or no, it is very evident to
anyone staying in Sydney or Melbourne, that,
substituting a plutocracy for an aristocracy,—
a moneyed class hovering on the outskirts of
the Government House party,—there is almost
the same society, shorn maybe of its culture,
but with its old vices and virtues. Never
believe that in this democratic community all
men are equal. Far from it. A leisured
class will be on the scene ere many years
have run their course, and there are already
three or four levels. Of course the transi-
tion is far more rapid than in older countries.
The Radical working-man, who in his poverty
lost no opportunity of badgering those in
authority, blossoms in a single "boom" into
a large contractor, and buys a mansion at
Potts Point, in the drawing-room of which

FRED KAYE.

his good lady forthwith hangs oil paint-
ings, and framed prints from the Christmas
Numbers. Some strange manners go hand in
hand with fine clothes down Potts Point way,
and perhaps we may be forgiven one little
anecdote illustrating this. A friend was
walking one day down Macleay Street, and
all but trod upon a little oxidised watch,
which he kept until an advertisement should
in due course appear in the next morning's
Herald. Sure enough, there was an offer of
one pound reward, and the address, a large
house close to the spot where he had picked
it up. By way of saving the owner the
expense of the reward, he took it back himself ; and the chatelaine almost snatched it
from him, with never a word of thanks but,
" Wait a minute, and I'll get the pound ! "
Blank surprise was the prevailing expression
on this Mrs. T.'s face, as her visitor politely

declined the munificent guerdon of honesty, and let himself out.

The sequel to which episode was, that it was related that same afternoon, at an At Home, "how a man brought the watch back this morning, and was quite rude when ma offered him the reward."

We should apologise for introducing so trivial an episode, did it not point a painful moral that need not be further dwelt upon.

In hospitality the colonial is a very Arab. It is open house, without so much as asking your name, in the bush ; and even in the cities, on the least excuse,—a letter of introduction from a half-forgotten acquaintance,—they give you of their best. Taking in the stranger, not by any means the "angel unawares" of St. Paul, often ends in their being hopelessly taken in themselves, as a large number of rascally adventurers from Europe have by means of forged credentials won their way into colonial society, and even married their heiresses. From somewhat frequent lessons, however, they are learning caution.

Another noticeable feature of life in the colonies is the child. Australian children are terribly in evidence. They seem to accompany their mother on her afternoon calls. They are taken to receptions and theatres, which they cannot possibly enjoy. Perhaps the explanation of this is to be sought in the retrenchment all round—of nurses as of civil servants.

It is not very generally understood at home that Australia is, so far as its citizens are concerned, a poor country just now, though this will not always be so, and nurses, like 'bus conductors, are reckoned an unnecessary luxury. *Ergo*, the mother must stay at home or take her olive-branches with her. Small blame to her for choosing the latter alternative. She takes them round on show, and is as proud of the spoilt, bumptious little brats as the Roman lady was of her two little prigs.

We are often asked—one does get some curious questions on returning after a long voyage—about the standard of education in the colonies. And, dismissing so serious a topic in as few words as possible, we should be inclined to say that education is far more widely diffused than at home, though highly cultured men are perhaps few and far between. Books are little read, save colonial editions of sensational fiction. *Trilby* had a good sale. But, on the whole, the bars do a better trade than the bookstalls, journalism is wretchedly underpaid, and sheep's brains fetch more than men's. The Sydney Free Library, of which mention has already been made, is often nearly empty.

On politics let us be equally brief. We happened to be in Sydney during the July election, when Parkes, Dibbs, and other prominent men lost their seats, and popular excitement ran high.

The crowds in King Street were so dense that it was exceedingly difficult to get to the theatre.

The working-man's vote rules the country, and the "man to save us" is he who promises to tax the classes and exempt the masses.

At that particular election, Mr. George Reid, a barrister of some ability, but of scarcely commanding presence, went to the country on the Free Trade question, and was returned with flying colours. His octogenarian adversary, on the other hand, who had been calling large Federation-meetings all the winter, lost his place, and has since been devoting himself to literary work. A little way retired premiers seem to affect!

The attitude of these autonomous colonies towards the mother country, if such terms can be used without suggestion of irony, is unequivocal.

Socially, as politically, great changes are coming over colonial life as the old order passes away; and future biographers will soon have to treat of the Australian race, and not of so many exiled Englishmen and their children's children.

Climate and the removal of many restraints will compass much; and although England will still be "home" to colonials of the fifth generation, they will have lost many of the family vices and a few of its virtues.

It seems impossible to quit the subject of

colonial traits without referring to their sport. The traditions of the land of their origin, and the climate of the land of their birth, make colonials born sportsmen. The widespread enthusiasm for cricket and football is remarkable. At intercolonial contests you may see little girls applauding good, or condemning faulty, combination with singular judgment.

At the last Sydney test football match, where we saw the 'Varsity defeat the "Pirates," with some capital play on either side, there must have been five thousand spectators in the enclosures.

Even golf, which the young lady in *Punch* was so surprised to find in an out-of-the-way place like Scotland, has found its way to the Southern Hemisphere; and there are several clubs at Sydney and Melbourne. It is noticeable, that in approach shots the ball must be taken very cleanly, it being impossible to cut out a divot on that coarse turf.

Shooting is chiefly confined to the "back-blocks," as the remoter districts are called. Our wallaby drive has already been mentioned. Round Sydney, it is chiefly a chance of a few gill birds or wonga-wonga pigeons by day, or an "opossum" or flying squirrel by night.

Fishing is a favourite sport in and around Sydney Harbour, and on one occasion some of the company braved the rolling Pacific in a cockleshell of a tugboat, and got very ill and caught nothing. There are quieter fishing grounds within the harbour, but winter is the wrong season for them.

Horse-racing is rather too popular, if anything, in the colonies. On one occasion in Melbourne, two of the company rode in an amateur handicap, and a voice from the crowd was heard to exclaim, " Those Gaiety boys ride better than they act!" Anyhow, most of us dropped money at Randwick and Flemington, and felt henceforth convinced that betting is the curse of the colonies. That it is the curse of the working-man out there is certain at anyrate. He plunges incorrigibly. Failure drives him to crime; success prompts him to drink.

At the same time, it must be admitted that at many a colonial racecourse things are far better ordered than at Epsom or Longchamps. The starting machine, the plainly numbered saddle-cloths, and the disposal of the course so that all present can see the race from start to finish—these are among the arrangements which are far in advance of our notions of comfort.

Homeward Bound

Homeward Bound

Adelaide—Albany—Colombo—Aden—The Canal—
Port Said—Naples—Gibraltar—The Bay—Ply·
mouth—The River.

ROUGH treatment we got, as already stated, from the Pacific, and several fair ones—and a few of the other kind—were laid low for some hours ; while Miss Hobson, Miss Kearney, Bradfield, and Ryley escaped by going overland as far as Adelaide, where we arrived early in the morning of the 28th.

And the *Austral*, bearing the new Governor, Sir Thomas Fowell Buxton, dropped anchor in Largs Bay almost with ourselves. While we were up in the city, a large shark was caught, but most of it, save a few teeth, had disappeared on the following day, when we returned; and the *Oruba* got under way and started across the troubled waters of the great Australian Bight.

We enjoyed splendid weather, however, and reached Albany late in the evening of 2nd November, leaving the same night, after we had taken in a small cargo of wool. Thus we had no opportunity of visiting this rising port, where so many fortune - seekers land every week for the goldfields, presently returning, far less sanguine, for the most part, than they landed. Still there are, doubtless, exceptions.

As soon as we had to face ten days of sea and sky in grim earnest, an Amusement-Committee was duly formed, and some excellent concerts, dances, and deck sports were got up. Even now one has vague memories of a fancy dress ball, in which a baby, a gold digger, Deadwood Dick, a Spanish girl, and some coons figured prominently.

The day after the ties in the sports were concluded—the prizes, by the way, being mostly won by the ship's officers—we sighted Ceylon, and anchored in the picturesque harbour of Colombo just before sunset, passing the outward-bound *Orizaba* just outside the breakwater.

We naturally made at once for the shore, which we reached in various craft, and several of us put up at that cool and comfortable hotel, the Grand Oriental. Alas for its seductive arcades! Alas for the persuasive rascals, with their spurious jewellery, ivory elephants, embroidered cloths, and lace!

Penniless we returned to our quarters on board, some to dive once more into the cash-box and rush ashore for more rubbish. Yet what delightful memories of beautiful Lanka, for all its pirates!

The evening drive in 'rickshaws, with myriads of fireflies breaking the swift-falling darkness; the drive at sunrise out to Mount Lavinia, and the delicious breakfast of unrivalled prawn curry provided there; the picturesque, overcrowded bazaars; the delightful Cinnamon Gardens, and the quaint old temples, with their images of Buddha in every conceivable posture, and the fantastic frescoed walls portraying the tortures of the damned — it seemed too much almost to crowd into one day; but the inexorable Blue Peter was up, as we could see through the telescope in the drawing-room of the hotel, and we must needs tear ourselves

away from all the life and din and bright-
ness, and get aboard. Only just in time,
too, for the screw was revolving again at
noon.

Just before leaving, we were ill-advised
enough to purchase a number of love-birds
and Ceylon birds like parrakeets, of gay
plumage but doubtful voice. This was done
in utter disregard of the kindly warnings of
our friendly butcher, and perhaps also out of
compassion for the sufferings of the saleable
feathered ones; and sure enough they had all
gone—where we had no wish to follow them
—within a few days.

After a week of very hot weather we
passed Aden, and entered the Red Sea the
same night. Here the temperature fell considerably, and overcoats came forth after a
long absence.

Early on the morning of the 23rd we lay

off old Suez, and were at once surrounded by dhows and boarded by more thieves selling photographs, figs, Turkish delight, lace from Malta, and stuffed parrot-fish and shells from Jaffa. By breakfast-time the last of these enterprising ones had been coaxed or thrown over the side, and we were entering the wonderful canal, with the desert on one side and a caravan of dromedaries on the other. Twice before reaching the lakes we had to tie-up to allow other vessels to pass. Kaye tried his hand at navigation, but no serious accident resulted. This was rather to Kaye's credit. So he says.

Port Said was reached before daybreak on the Sunday; and during the three or four hours in which the ship's side was transformed into a scene out of Dante's *Inferno*, black demons shrieking and dancing in the weird light of charcoal fires and paraffin lamps, we ran ashore, and were hopelessly robbed for the third time. Donkeys were hired, and we rode in parties out to the Arab quarter.

Woodhouse, otherwise Wood-O, needed all his skill in horsemanship to keep his saddle; and while he fared badly, many of us, unable to ride at all, came off even worse. We do not mean this in the literal sense; and to the honour of the company be it recorded that no fall is known to have occurred. The beggars that pestered us in the streets proved an unmitigated nuisance. One man with a little boy approached Kaye, and prevailed upon his sympathetic nature to part with what small change he had about him, by the following piteous appeal:—"Me poor man, sir. Me very poor man. Dis little child, he no fader, no moder. Him very poor little child. Him my child." The obvious contradiction of this man's statement did not become apparent until after another rogue had tried the same dodge. We need scarcely say that the efforts of No. 2 were unsuccessful.

Those who wandered about without the services of a so-called guide were the lucky ones, and are to be congratulated on their escape from these ill-conditioned birds of prey. One unfortunate member of our company found, on arriving back at the boat, that he had paid the guide of his party twice over. The chief items of purchase were Egyptian cigarettes; and for a week afterwards the woe-begone American straight-cut was taboo in the smoke-room. The streets of Port Said are most interesting; and we would fain have lingered longer, gazing at the novel sights, admiring on the one hand, but not infrequently disgusted beyond measure. Here, a tame pelican was to be seen strutting proudly in front of the police-station or guard - house, indifferent to the ravenous mongrels prowling about in search of some such wholesome delicacy; at another place a boy was offering for sale two live salmon-coloured flamingoes, for the modest sum of half a crown the pair. One of the authors felt sorely tempted to make the purchase; but being already the proud pos-sessor of an Australian parrot and an enter-taining East Indian ape, both of which he hoped to get home alive, he thought better of what might have proved a doubtful acquisition. In all probability these flamin-goes would have followed their feathered relations the Ceylon love - birds, whose premature decease we have already re-corded.

Our cabins took some time to get straight.

Boxes of Turkish delight, and nougat; pipes; cigarettes, laces, shawls, and Moorish slippers littered the floor in thriftless profusion. The roll of the Mediterranean soon awoke us to the stern fact that we were leaving behind us the sunny land of Egypt, with all its gay sights and strange fascination. Would that the " Gaiety Girl" had chosen to exhibit her charms to the *fellaheen* of Cairo and Alexandria ! She might still have been able to write on her banner the memorable words of the greatest of Egypt's ravishers : " *Veni, vidi, vici.*" But it was not to be. The good ship *Oruba* was bearing us swiftly homewards; and at each new dawn everyone felt that, after all, we were glad to return home.

The remainder of our journey is quite devoid of interest, and may be dismissed in a few words.

In the Mediterranean we encountered cold weather and rough seas. On the second evening after leaving Port Said we coasted along the unpromising shores of Crete.

Next day we passed the *Orient*; and on the next we lay for an hour under the shadow of Vesuvius, where several of the company, being wanted at home by Mr. Edwardes, left by tender. Short as was our stay, it enabled some Neapolitans with an eye to business to cheat us out of what little Colombo, Suez, and Poit Said had left.

On the last day of November we passed through the Straits of Gibraltar, after lying a very short time off the town itself; and the snow on the Sierra Nevada, the first snow we had seen for so many months, suggested a curious coincidence. The last snow that we had looked on had been on that other Sierra Nevada in the Far West.

Along the coast of Portugal the weather was much warmer. Off Finisterre we dipped to the *Ormuz*, and ran through the bay in calm weather.

Several landed at Plymouth and finished the journey by rail, but the rest of us preferred completing the round by sea, and went up Channel in cold, unpleasant winds. Beachy Head, Eastbourne, Hastings, Dungeness, and the Goodwins were passed on the 4th, when we lay for some hours in low water off Thames Head, and finally reached Tilbury early on the 5th.

Thus ended our delightful trip of four hundred and thirty - one days Round the World with *A Gaiety Girl*.

MORRISON AND GIBB, PRINTERS, EDINBURGH